B

DJ Charpentier

As always and again...

To Pat, my forever partner;

Also

My daughters, Jess and Lori

And my Mom & Dad;

Thanks for the memories.

Other Books by DJ Charpentier

As Luck Would Have It...Changing Your Mind

A Practical Guide to Retirement

Table of Contents

"Only put off until tomorrow what you are willing to have left undone."

Pablo Picasso (1881-1973)

Preface

Childhood friendships are a lasting thing. People that you have known since an early age know things about you that no one else knows or will ever know. Even after years of being apart, there is a bond that exists among these early life partners that is unlike any other relationship you will have in your life. These are the people that witnessed your growing up...your maturity. They saw the mistakes you made and have somehow forgiven you and you have forgiven them.

There is such a group in my own life. They know who they are and they are not the inspiration for this story. We met in elementary school and still meet periodically for dinner, thanks to Grace. I mention Grace because she brought us together, the second time. Grace's parents' home was the place we all met as young teenagers. We met there to hang out. We met there to have parties in the basement. The music of our times played on the Hi-Fi constantly. We fell in love with and by that music. The music has great meaning to me and thus all the chapter titles and music references throughout this writing.

Every life situation brings to mind a song title or musical line. They are the bylines of life. They are also one of life's true inspirations. My musical friend, Dave, regards song titles as one of the most difficult things to come up with...the most difficult being a band name. It's true...how do you describe yourself as a band by a name...difficult at best. There have been some classic band names such as the classic misspelling of The Beatles, and the Rolling Stones, or The Moody Blues. Hear one guitar lick, one strike of a chord and you know who made it. It is their sound...the sounds of our youth. So I humbly thank all of those great songwriters that came up with those titles and those lines that I refer to throughout this book.

But back to Grace...she was a friend to us all...all the people of my youth. We did not see each other for a long time. Life has a way of doing that. You get busy doing other things like getting married and having and raising kids. It just all gets in the way. In the middle of all that, Grace died. Of course we all went and met up at the wake. We vowed to get together and we did...and we still do. Thank you, Grace.

Every once in a while we get together for pizza, or dinner, or whatever and just talk. It goes on for a long time...every time and it always feels good. I believe, and it is confirmed by these friends, that we all grew up in a great time, in a safe neighborhood, and all in all had a great childhood. We did not fear what parents and children fear today. I feel sorry for them in a way. They have missed out...we did not.

So, thanks to all of you...you know who you are. Let's get together soon. May this serve as an invitation to stop by. I want to see you.

These people are part of what made my life and influence my thinking. It was all for the good. I would not be the person I am today without them.

I mention all of this because this book is such a story, but it does not turn out as well.

DJ Charpentier

Chapter 1: You've Lost That Lovin' Feelin'

Reggie felt like he had been in a school of one level or another for most of his life. His earliest memories were of the Catholic elementary school in his old neighborhood. Sister Gregory ruled her charges with an iron hand from lining up in the morning in the school yard to the highly regimented Safety Patrols that led us homeward in the afternoon.

Sister Gregory's first grade class was taught to line up, as soon as the school bell sounded, in a specific place in the school yard near their entry door for the first and fourth grades and next to the fifth and sixth grade lines. Mom had walked him to school the first couple of days, but after that he was on his own. She was not neglecting him because there were others walking and it was no problem to make his way safely to school, home for a hot lunch, back to school for the afternoon session, and then line up and walk with the Safety Patrol along the main street after school back home again. Things were different back then and the world seemed somehow safer.

These days, no self respecting mother in his school's neighborhood would allow their child to walk to school. Some let their precious bundles of joy ride the school bus, but most carried their children to school in the suburban assault vehicles (SUV's), most so high that the children had difficulty getting out. The smaller children had to be lifted out of the back seat to the ground level. This dance was repeated in the afternoon to release their children from school. The upper-grade, student-led Safety Patrols did not exist anymore.

Sister Gregory's class was a model of efficiency. The first thing Reggie remembered doing was the whole class counting from one to one hundred reading from the huge chart in front of the room as Sister Gregory pointed to each number with her long pointer stick. As the year went on, it was an honor to be chosen to lead the class in this activity. Reggie had been chosen in-turn for this duty with the other members of the class.

The counting had become more complicated as the year passed. Counting all the way to one hundred was a celebrated milestone. Counting by two's, three's, four's, five's...etc. prepared everyone for the multiplication tables that would come in future grades. When Reggie had become a teacher, thirty years later, this practice had been ridiculed as ancient and barbaric. It was ironic that by the time he became a principal fifteen years later, it had become innovative again. That was the way of most programs...put a new spin on it and the practice was heralded as a gift from heaven. Sister Gregory had been that and had grounded his knowledge of mathematics from the start.

The shiny floors and the desks in rows, bolted to the floor were the ilk of grades one through four...the first floor in Reggie's elementary school. By the time he had moved to the second floor for grades five through eight, new desks with flip-top lids were the fashion. These were later banned as being hazardous. The little fingers of delicate children could be crushed by the falling desktops...it never happened to anyone he knew, but the horror of mashed little digits was the nightmare of parents. Reggie always thought they were a great idea for keeping things organized and from a teacher's perspective; not having any distracting things on a student's desk. What goes around comes around. Now there were no distracting books on a child's desk, they all resided inside a student's laptop or tablet.

'Haven't I seen that black BMW before?' Reggie's reminiscent thoughts were interrupted by the erratic traffic flow. Yes, that's the one that passed me in a blur near the Connecticut line and there he goes again. He must have stopped for a latte and was now trying to make up the time.

Reggie was driving south on I-95 through Connecticut having left his condo in Rhode Island that morning headed for Bethany Beach, Delaware. The BMW could not have stopped just for a plain coffee...not with that car! He must be in a hurry to get to work...poor bastard. Work your fingers to the bone to buy a fast car so you can drive fast to work because you are late...not even time to enjoy that fancy cup of coffee. What a rat race!

Reggie's Rhode Island condo had served him well. He didn't want to sell it. He was only going to Bethany for the summer. His nephew, James, was watching it for him. The 20 year old was taking summer classes at Providence College. His parents, Reggie's sister and brother-in-law, lived in Narragansett. The commute into the city would be much quicker for the nephew from Reggie's place in Cranston. Besides, he liked having someone to look after the place.

There would be no more drives to work for Reggie...neither fast nor slow. Last week he said goodbye to all of that. Two retirements and that would be his last. It was somewhat bittersweet as he looked down the vacant corridors of the school for the last time, but this was the prize, the golden apple. Retirement was supposed to be the dream of every working man, right? But, what would he do now? He had made it to the top of the hill. What comes after that?

These had been his thoughts as he stood at the intersection of the school's main corridors for the last time. Everyone had gone home. It was summer vacation now and only the occasional teacher came in to do some work in their rooms and the custodians worked summer hours. Everyone was gone for the day and the building was silent. Reggie Slater was alone with his thoughts.

High school had been a blur with part-time work and some playing time on the baseball team. He had been a decent defensive player but needed hitting instruction. He could have become better but because of the work, he had never really got into the after school relish of a high school student. Reggie regretted that. There must have been something there that he had missed. He would never know. No regrets per se but just the wonder of what else was there and what had happened to all of those boys, now aged men that he had spent four years with.

It was the era of Vietnam when he finished high school and many of his fellow graduates had gone into the service. The draft was still very much of a reality in those days. How many of them had served, died, or been injured in that war? Where were they all now? All those questions...probably never will be answered. The high school had closed two years after he left. There were no reunions. Maybe no one wanted to know. Maybe it was better that way.

The only one he knew about for sure was Ted. Ted had gone to Europe after his first year in college and never came back. He was killed sleeping on a beach in Italy by some nut with an ax. There was a wake and a funeral...Reggie just couldn't bring himself to go. He still thought about Ted. He didn't want to end up like Ted so soon after retirement splattered all over I-95 south by a speeding BMW. It was a wonder more people didn't die on the highway, the way they drove.

His exit for the Tappan Zee Bridge would be coming up soon. He'd have to pay attention because the GPS always wanted to direct him to the George Washington Bridge because it was the shorter route to Bethany Beach, Delaware, his final destination today. But the traffic was often heavier that way and the Tappan Zee to the Garden State Parkway was his favored route.

He had driven this route several times. Bethany Beach was a favorite vacation spot with its small town atmosphere and great beach. He had tried Ocean City, Maryland, but it was a bit busy for his taste but nice to visit at times for a dose of excitement. There was the exit ahead. He took it and entered I-287 for the Tappan Zee.

The conventional wisdom provided by all the retirement gurus was not to make any radical moves soon after retirement; especially buying a retirement home in your favorite vacation spot. So, as the advisors recommended, he would rent. Reggie had decided over the last year that he would go down to Bethany and rent for a few months and see how he liked it. He liked it fine for a two or three week vacation but would it be different to live there permanently? That's what he needed to find out.

He had always been a tourist when he visited Bethany. Now he wanted to get a place for a few months and really live there; submerge himself in the town. He wanted to get to know some people. Not vacationers but people who lived there all through the year. People he could make a life with. As the retirement people called it, your next phase.

The silence of the car brought him back to his thoughts of standing in that corridor alone at the end of his career...the end of his career...it was only last week. Over twenty years as a teacher and principal also over twenty years in the Air National Guard before that...what was that... 21 years...a statute of limitations? The National Guard had been good to him, kept him out of Vietnam. He was lucky in that draft lottery. It had been the only lottery he had ever won. He drew a draft number of 7...that's right 7...as in *'learn an Asian language you're going to Vietnam'*...7...geez. He had no regrets about missing any of that mess. The National Guard had saved him from that.

The school system had been good to him as well. He had held the positions of elementary school teacher, middle school teacher, assistant principal, and finally principal. It was a good career and he could leave with a clear conscience...again, no regrets. He had met many young people and maybe he had influenced a few to do good or maybe even great things. Maybe he would see it someday...the success of his students but most likely not and only hope that they were better human beings for being present in his classroom.

He passed smoothly along I-287 and across the Tappan Zee. It was a beautiful spot, the Tappan Zee. A wide part of the Hudson River below West Point and above New York City with steep banks on each side and the wide Hudson flowing below; he always enjoyed the amazing sight. The evidence of pilings being driven for the new bridge was evident and significant progress had been made since he last passed this way. The drive on I-287 was brief and not clogged by traffic and soon Reggie came upon his exit and headed south on the Garden State Parkway through New Jersey.

The first rest area, located in the center median of the highway, was his usual stop. He took the exit on the left and drifted into the parking lot. He dodged cars in the busy rest stop and headed into the food court. The rest area food available ran the gamut just like most mall food courts in American these days. There was pizza, subs, coffee, the sunglass kiosk; all anchored by one of the chicken/burger joints in this case Burger King. Reggie first hit the men's room and then took his place in line and ordered a small burger/fries/drink combo meal. He sat at one of the plastic table and chair sets to watch the cars and the people pass by while he ate.

The roadside rest stop was like most on the American highways. All steel and glass, the spacious building was cold yet inviting, giving comfort to weary travelers who were always interesting to watch. There were the usual commuters who could always be spotted by their hurried attitude. Nothing slowed them down including the gas attendants or food counter clerks. The expectation was the lightening speed of a NASCAR pit stop, but the attendants and clerks worked at their own measured pace. The commuters just paced and waited; then raced back onto the highway, like they had lost positions in a race.

Then there were the traveling families, some practiced at the art of travel some not so much. These nomads extracted their children out of heavily packed cars and through the rest rooms. They patiently explained the food choices to the young ones but the young children were not easily adaptable to, nor satisfied with, the choices always wanting something else that was not available. There was the inevitable crying fit that resulted in some tiff between Mom and Dad, a meal eaten in silence, children stowed back into the car asking, "How much longer?"

Reggie watched all these shows play out as he finished his meal and then zigzagged his way across the lot to his car. He pulled up to the gas pumps and turned his credit card over to the attendant. The attendants had to pump your gas in New Jersey. No "pump your own." Here, Reggie thought, it was the way it used to be everywhere and the way he liked it. He made small talk with the gas attendant and when finished, merged his way back onto the highway.

The traffic was light today and he was making good time. He soon found himself at the junction of the New Jersey Turnpike, passed through the toll, and took the truck/car lanes southbound. Last year the traffic had been tough along this route. The turnpike had been undergoing a widening for the past couple of years. Now that the work was done, the highway had been repaved and widened. There were three lanes for cars and three lanes for cars/trucks making for six lanes in each direction. The highway narrowed and the car and car/truck lanes merged in the southern portion towards the Delaware Memorial Bridge but the traffic thinned out by then and moved along as smoothly as it was moving now.

As he drove along, Reggie thought about taking that last look down each of the now vacant corridors of the school building. He breathed deeply and turned to go back to his office. On the way he passed the portraits of each of the staff groups taken with each of the past school principals including himself. There would be more over the years. Eventually, someone would pass these photos and think of them as they thought of those stiff-collared, bronze-toned portraits adorning the myriad of school corridors depicting their founders, headmasters, and the like. He would barely be remembered, if at all, and fade into the school's history as all of the students, teachers, and staff would as well. Reggie was thinking, "Nothing is forever," as he entered the school principal's office.

Over the last few years he would have thought of it as his office but as of today...it no longer was his. Gone were all of the personal mementoes and pictures that had adorned the walls. The naked nails and pins on the wall would now hold someone else's memories, albeit temporarily. He removed the school's master key from his key ring and placed it in the middle of the blank blotter on the desk. Reggie walked slowly from his office closing the locked door behind him. He set the alarm code in the outer office and exited the building through the main doors listening for the telltale locking click behind him. He stopped to check that the doors were secure, got in his car, and drove away...for the last time.

The slowing cars in front of him focused his attention. They were approaching the Delaware Memorial Bridge. Cars were entering the highway from other roads slowing the pace as they made their way up the bridge's incline. It was a bit foggy at the top today and the visibility was limited. He glided down the other side and passed through the EZ Pass toll lane. He made his way a bit further down I-95 and took the exit for State Road 1 south.

State Road 1 in Delaware had been completed a few years ago. Before that the primary route to the Delaware beaches has been Rt. 113. The old Rt. 113 ran through many small towns along the way and had become especially difficult in the summer. To facilitate development and the route to the beach, the Delaware DOT had graciously built this new road and established a toll system for the beach destined throngs from northern New Jersey and Philadelphia. This way was much smoother and traffic-free than the old route making passage to Reggie's destination and his future swift.

Chapter 2: Surfin' Safari

Pulling into Bethany Beach always provided a feeling of peace and contentment. It was just a matter of being there. Reggie thought those feelings were what he sought for his retirement. He had endured the pressure cooker long enough. It was time to relax. So, Reggie headed for the place that had always provided that feeling for him, Bethany Beach.

The roads had turned rural south of Dover Air Force Base passing through corn and other assorted vegetable fields. He often had stopped at the roadside mom and pop vegetable stands but not right now. First, he would settle into the motel efficiency he had rented for a week, gather some supplies, and take a look around town.

Bethany was not the seaside village that time forgot but neither was it the thriving tourist metropolis like Rehoboth to the north or Ocean City to the south. Bethany was more of a family vacation spot focused on the beach. If you wanted the hoopla, go north or go south, but here in Bethany it was the feel of the sand between your toes and the crashing of the surf that was the focus...and everyone, including Reggie, seemed to like to like it that way.

There were quicker routes but Reggie liked approaching Bethany from the north because it provided the best views and brought on that "Peaceful Easy Feeling". Water was on both sides of the road now, the Atlantic Ocean on his left and the inland tidal basins on this right. There were pricey, high-rise condo units on both sides...higher priced on the left of course kissing the Atlantic beaches. There were gated communities protecting the townhouses and condos of the rich and not so famous. These were not in his price range, not even close. He had made arrangements to rent that motel efficiency unit for a week on the edge of town while he looked for something more permanent. He wouldn't be looking at condos in this area.

Reggie passed the Delaware Army National Guard Training Site on his right as he entered the Town of Bethany Beach with its olive drab helicopter on a pedestal fifty-feet high looking like it was about to make a combat run on the beach a few blocks down across the street. The helicopter was probably an old, hollowed-out wreck that looked like its old self on the outside but really wasn't much more than an empty shell of the deadly combat weapon it had been. It now stood guard over the beach, a silent sentential.

He slowed to a stop at the light at the top of Garfield Parkway. He could see the wooden Chief Little Owl totem pole on the corner with the eagle head on top and a likeness of Chief Little Owl himself welcoming or maybe warning all who came. Looking down Garfield, one could see the shops and restaurants lining each side with the angled parking; the street sloping down to the band shell in the distance on the beach plaza. He knew the boardwalk and the beach were just beyond the band shell and from his position he could just make out the waters of the Atlantic. This was the town commerce center for Bethany vacationers.

The light turned green and he moved forward. His motel was just a couple of blocks south and on the left. Reggie put on his directional and moved into the turn lane. He had to stop to let the traffic pass and he pulled into the short drive next to the Bethany Shores motel office. The place was probably new in the 1960's and had been renovated a couple of times since. The present motif was white with blue trim. Each room had a darker blue door with a tarnished bronze number affixed. He parked at a spot labeled "check-in" and went into the office.

The clerk on duty introduced himself as Larry. He looked to be about forty and Larry volunteered that his Mom and Dad owned the place and he was just helping out.

"Do you have a reservation?" asked Larry.

"I do," answered Reggie and he handed Larry the confirmation e-mail he had received.

"Do you still want the efficiency for the week," Larry inquired.

"Let's start with a week for now. I'm looking for a place for the summer so let's go day by day after that. I'll let you know."

"OK," said Larry, "Let's get you signed in.

Larry filled out the rental agreement. It occurred to Reggie that he had probably been helping out his parents for awhile now and would continue the easy dependent life.

Larry led him down to room twelve, four down from the office. The motel was a two-story affair with what looked to be about thirty rooms with the office and living quarters on one end where Larry, no doubt, lived with his parents.

"The kitchenette is to the back and there's the bathroom. You can take the parking spot right out front. If you have any visitors, have them park in one of the visitors' spots. "

Larry's quick tour was over and he left Reggie to unpack. Reggie moved his car to the parking spot with the yellow twelve painted on the asphalt and took his two suitcases and four boxes from the car inside. He made quick work of stacking the boxes in the corner and putting the two suitcases on the racks provided. That done, he went into the bathroom and freshened up, hanging his toiletry bag on the hook next to the sink. He was home, for now.

The sink and tub/shower were blue as was the floor tile. The walls were painted white but the paint was thick and had been other colors in the past. Finishing up he moved out into the "open concept" bedroom/kitchen/dining area. It was not much bigger than a large master bedroom with a built in counter at one end with an apartment sized stove/microwave and sink with a metal table and chairs in between to make the space function as an efficiency unit. The white with blue trim paint continued into the bedroom with a grey carpet that had seen better days. The once white ceiling made of twelve inch acoustic tiles completed the décor.

Having "moved in" Reggie returned to his car to make a market run to set-in a few supplies. He thought that he might drive through the town to see the sights. He took the side road next to the motel and headed toward the beach. He had gone two short blocks when the street ended and he had to turn left or right. Left was toward town and he went that way. There was some traffic in late June but not what it would be in a couple of weeks when the summer season officially kicked off. He noticed a diner he had never seen before on his right. It was on the beach block but faced the street. The façade was completely redone in a fifties-style diner with chrome and red accents. A neon "Breakfast Served All Day" sign burned in the window. The name read Stan & Ollie's. Reggie guessed it was a take-off on the old comedy duo of Stan Laurel and Oliver Hardy. The place looked interesting. He would have to remember for tomorrow morning...it was easily within walking distance from the motel.

Reggie reached the other end of Garfield Parkway from the Totem Pole and was now next to the band shell on his right. He took a left on Garfield away from the beach toward Route 1. There, heading up the slight incline from the shoreline, was the town of Bethany Beach. Mango's, one of his favorite lunch spots, was at the beach on the band shell square. The bricked band shell square held several white benches for watching performances on the stage. The boardwalk went north and south along the dunes off the square. There were the same benches lining the beach railing along the boardwalk. Various shops were in the buildings on each side with the world famous local Grotto's Pizza across the square from Mango's and next to Stan & Ollie's.

Going up the street the smell of French fries drifted into the car from the left side of the street on the corner across the street from Grotto's Pizza. DB Fries doled them out by the bucket and the people lined up for the golden brown deep fried spuds. His mouth watered a bit as he thought of those large buckets of golden fries with salt clinging to their shiny hot lengths.

The Frog House, Parker House Restaurant, the Broadway themed diner and the tourist's shop in between; he had frequented them all over the years but now he really wanted to get to know them as friends and not just as a visitor. As he passed, a Dad was passing soft-serve ice cream cones to his wife and the two children. The look of delight on the children's faces made him smile.

His former visits had been made as escapes from the day-to-day pressures of the job. He had dabbled in attendance at the restaurants and shops and had never really made any friends nor even mild acquaintances. He wanted to change that. He wanted to learn the shop owner's names. He wanted bartenders to know his "usual" drink. He wanted to know the people of this town in order to decide if he wanted to live here, not merely visit.

He pulled his car into a small parking lot on the right about half-way up the street. The signs on each parking spot warned that parking was for the Town Market Only and violators would be prosecuted. Reggie wondered if there was some sort of torture chamber in the basement to deal with those who overstayed their welcome in the lot...this was some sort of high level security stuff.

Reggie went into the small market and filled a small plastic basket with essential supplies for his very efficient kitchen and approached the counter to check out. "Hello, Freda," He greeted the clerk, by the name she advertised on her embroidered shirt.

She gave him a half smile and said, "Allo," in some sort of eastern European accent, totaled his order, and made change. She placed his items into three plastic bags and handed them to him with an accented, "Dank You." He was dismissed as she moved on to the next customer; so much for making new friends.

Reggie drove back to the motel and parked in number twelve. He unloaded his groceries, made a cup of tea, and sat at the table to take stock. He had left Rhode Island and everything was taken care of there. His retirement check was being directly deposited into his account, so he would always have money. Cash he could get from any ATM. His nephew, James, was watching his place so there were no worries there. Rhode Island was on the back burner.

So, he was in Bethany Beach settled into the Bethany Shores Motel for at least a week. Now what? Yesterday he was Reggie Slater, elementary school principal, holder of a master's degree, etc. etc. So today he was Reggie Slater, 60 year old, retired...what?

"I guess that part of the resume is open," he said aloud. "Let's see what tomorrow brings."

Reggie made a sandwich from the supplies he had bought and ate it at the small table in his motel room. He stretched out on the bed and watched some TV and eventually dosed off.

---***---

Reggie awoke not quite sure where he was. He could see sunlight coming in through the front window and he could hear some traffic beginning to build on Route 1 outside his door. He came to realize that he was in Bethany and he realized he would have to find a place for the summer away from the busy highway. He showered, dressed, and waved to Larry working the desk as he headed, walking, down the side street to Stan & Ollie's.

He was walking at a good pace and enjoying the morning air. He could detect the scent of the sea and it breathed new life into him. There was a slight mist that Reggie was sure would soon burn off as the almost summer sun burned through the clouds. There were small cottages and some larger residential homes on either side of the street as he walked in the quiet of the morning. Most had driveways with two or three cars. Rental signs adorned most building with realty company logos and their phone number advertising a property for sale or rent.

Many of the homes here were private property, but due to their closeness to the beach, they were expensive. The owners tended to rent them out when they were not here to help pay the mortgage and taxes. Many were rented now, but come July 1st the owner's families would move in for the July/August months. Mom and the kids would set up at "the beach house" and Dad would return to the city to work. He would return on weekends and for a two-week stint sometime during the summer. Other than that, Mom and the kids would bask in the sun at the beach and enjoy the summer community life of Bethany. The most popular time that whole families would be in residence would be the month of July and the July 4th weekend would be the highlight of the summer. The Labor Day weekend was also popular, but more as a celebration of the summer passed.

Reggie reached the end of the side street and Saw Stan & Ollie's diagonally across the intersection. He made his way to the front door and stepped inside. The chrome and red façade décor continued from the outside front, through the door, and into the dining room. The diner was done in the old railroad car style, but it was much bigger inside. In front of him was a large space with a dining room to each side. There were red vinyl booths along the walls of each dining room with six free-standing tables in addition to the booths. There must have been about ten booths and with the six tables in each of the dining rooms many patrons could be seated.

In the center of the space was a horseshoe shaped bar area. The bar area had high backed wooden stools with leather padding set against a meticulously crafted gleaming wood bar with red leather facing. The back of the bar was also showed high quality carpentry work with mirrors and an assortment of liquor. The liquor was now covered with a sheet and well, it seemed a bit early for that anyway. Most of the tables and booths were filled even at this early hour so Reggie took a seat in one of the open stools at the bar.

"Good Morning," the waitress in a black and white check poodle skirt and white blouse said that had suddenly appeared before him on the other side of the bar, "Would you like coffee?"

she continued and she put a white mug in front of him and started to pour from the pot in her other hand.

"Thank you, yes," Reggie responded to the brilliant smile in front of him. The waitress's name tag read 'Lexie' so he tried the friendly approach.

"And good morning to you, Lexie," as she finished pouring, "Thanks, Lexie." She looked at him as if memorizing his face. In addition to the uniform clothing she wore, Lexie had brown, shoulder length hair; that gleaming smile; and green eyes. She was a pleasant sight to start the day.

"I don't think I've seen you in here before."

"Well, you're right. I've been to Bethany Beach many times before but I've never come down this end and no, I've never been in here…but it does seem to be where the locals all come to for breakfast," Reggie concluded looking around at the filled tables and booths with a mixture of couples and groups.

"I thought I hadn't seen you before, I'm good with faces. The locals do come in here for breakfast, lunch, and dinner. Stan & Ollie, the owners of the place, are returning locals themselves so everybody knows them and they come in for that but mostly they come in for the food…and to see each other. It's sort of the local gathering place and the place that opens the earliest around here."

Sounds like a good local place," said Reggie, "and "Hi there, Lexie. My name is Reggie," and he extended his hand across the bar. Lexie shook his hand with a good firm grip and gave him another of those brilliant smiles. She wasn't a young girl. He guessed her age to be mid-thirties but she kept herself well with her hair carefully coifed and soft pink nail polish. He did not see a wedding ring.

"I won't forget, Reggie. Like I said, I never forget a face," Lexie said while handing him a menu. "Pick out what you want and I'll be back in a sec after I pour some coffees down the bar," and she moved swiftly pouring as she went and making light conversation.

Reggie looked over the menu decided on the #2, two eggs/hash/potatoes. As he put the menu down on the bar and put the coffee mug to his lips, Lexie appeared in front of him laying the coffee pot on the bar.

"What'll it be?" she asked, pen and pad in hand.

"I'll have a #2, over easy, Lexie," Reggie requested.

"Cumin' right up," and she poured more coffee into his cup and scurried away before he could say anything else.

As he waited, he noticed that many patrons were dressed in t-shirts and pocketed work shirts with company logos silk screened or embroidered on them now telling each other to "Have a nice Day," and "Catch you later," as a signal they had to get going. Still others with open collars and with ties sitting at other tables lingered. These would be the bosses and supervisors planning the interactions of their day.

"Here you go," it was Lexie again. This time delivering his breakfast; but she didn't scurry off. "So, are you in town for long?" she asked.

"I'm here for the summer. I just retired."

"Aren't you a bit young for that?"

"Very kind of you but I'm not that young. I was in the military and then was a school principal so I have been working for awhile."

"Where are you staying?"

"Right now I'm staying at the Bethany Shores motel just up the street. I walked down this morning."

"We just have a few parking spots out front so most people either walk or park at the beach in front of the bandstand but they start charging for parking after 8:00 so people get going by then," Lexie informed him. "Are you going to stay at Bethany Shores all summer," she continued.

"No, just for a week; I'm looking for something to lease by the month until at least Labor Day."

"You better move fast. Most of the long-term rentals here are not commercial but privately owned and already locked in for most of the summer. The realty companies handle most of the rentals so if I were you I would contact somebody today."

"I'll do that. Thanks, Lexie," and she hurried off to greet another arriving customer.

Reggie ate his breakfast, which was excellent...and the hash seemed homemade not out-of-a-can mush. Lexie was busy so he left a generous tip and she waved...and he waved as he went out into the now bright sunlight.

He decided to walk back through the town up Garfield Parkway. There were a few people on the street and a few early joggers and walkers headed for the beach. The throngs would come at about ten o'clock but for now the town was mostly quiet.

Reggie passed Grotto Pizza and then took the turn up Garfield. DB French Fries was locked and silent. He looked in the windows of Fisher's Popcorn. He would have to stop by later and pick up some of the caramel corn...his mouth watered just thinking about it. They made it fresh on the premises and a tub of Fisher's caramel corn was a must during any visit to Bethany Beach. The stainless steel bins were empty now and the counters were silent but he could still smell the caramel wafting through the air. He walked along moving up the hill past the Parker House and Frog House restaurants.

Reggie crossed the street by the bank and walked another block to Route 1. He nodded to Chief Little Owl, turned left, and walked the block and a half back to the Bethany Shores Motel parking lot. Before he went in his room he noticed a realty/rental office just across the street. The name on the sign read Blue Sky Realty. He waved to Larry sitting in the office through the large plate glass window as he walked past.

The rest of the day was wasted by Reggie. And no one bugged him about it. It was a good feeling.

Chapter 3: Start Me Up!

"Good morning, Lexie." Reggie had walked down to Stan & Ollie's for breakfast after a good night's rest even after napping all day. He felt revived and ready to begin again.

"Good morning, Reggie," and again she flashed that welcoming smile. "Will it be the usual?"

Reggie didn't think that a one-time order constituted "the usual" but maybe other town folk got stuck in a rut. "How about we go off the rails and have bacon this morning," Reggie quipped. Lexie poured him a mug of coffee and sped off.

The regular crowd seemed to occupy their usual places...he wondered if they were assigned...like seats in a classroom? It was before 8:00 and the place was buzzing with chatter. He noticed there was a man in uniform with colonel's wings on his collar and scrambled eggs on the brim of his cap which was on the table in front of him. Must be the local police chief, he thought.

"Here you go," it was Lexie with his breakfast and she refilled his mug. "That guy is Chief Lamar Stanton," she volunteered. "He's the local top-cop; comes in here all the time. He's really nice and everybody likes him. He's ex-state police and only been chief here a few years but he knows everybody and everything that's going on."

"He seems popular, but a bit young to be retired. He looks younger than I am."

"The Staties (as the State Police are affectionately known) can retire after 20 years on the job. He was a detective and put in about 25 years and then got the job here. Looking for a quieter life,

I guess, moved here with his wife, Elsie, after he got the job. Elsie was no stranger to Bethany though. She had spent many summers here with her family when she was younger."

"Sounds like a good gig if you can get it."

"Seems to be working out for them; got to go." and she went to pour coffee at other tables.

It was just 8:00 and men were getting up and moving off to work. There was a small group at the table with the Chief. They were all leaning in and seemed to be discussing something of importance to all of them. Reggie finished his breakfast and the caucus with the Chief broke up.

Reggie paid the bill and exchanged, "Have a nice day," with Lexie. He walked up the side street back toward the motel. There were now people sitting on their porches and decks reading the newspaper and sipping coffee. That was the peaceful morning moment he was looking for. Instead of going back to his room, he crossed the busy Route 1, and headed for Blue Sky Realty.

---***---

Reggie opened the door to Blue Sky Realty and stepped into a bright space with a chest-high counter in front of him. A receptionist was on the phone in front of him and on the other side of the counter.

"How can I help you?" she asked hanging up the telephone. She was professionally dressed in a red dress that accented her figure with carefully applied make-up and short black hair. Thinking about the beach, she would definitely accent the beach in a swimsuit.

"I'm looking for someone to help me with a long-term rental."

"I think Rachael is in the office. I'll check," she said spinning in her chair and going through the open doorway behind her and disappearing around the corner. Reggie's original physical observation was confirmed as she walked down the hall. She returned in a moment with the supposed Rachael in tow.

"Good morning. I'm Rachael Short," said a well proportioned forty-something woman dressed in a light gray business suit extending her hand. The suit was tight-fitting exposing the proper amount of cleavage to attract attention. There were small frills extending from her sleeves.

"I'm Reggie. Nice to meet you Ms. Short," he said extending his hand.

"Please, call me Rachael," she said shaking his hand. "Tammy here tells me you're looking for a long-term rental. It's a bit late in the season but let's see if we can find something that suits your needs. Follow me," she said opening the gate in the counter.

Reggie followed her down the corridor to her office admiring her walk and the legs all the way down to the high heels that supported those shapely legs extending from the skirt of her suit. Rachael turned into a small office and went behind her desk. She straightened her skirt and sat in the high backed office chair.

"Now, what are you looking for?" she inquired taking a form from a tray on the side of her desk. She also centered a legal pad on her desk with a fresh page for notes.

"I'm looking for a rental for at least until Labor Day and perhaps beyond. I only need one bedroom, a kitchen, and sitting area. A porch or balcony would be great." Rachael wrote notes on her pad and made check marks on the form.

"OK and let's fill in some personal information." Reggie provided name, address, credit information, and several other items. Rachael filled in the form.

They discussed price and some other particular issues concerning a possible rental. Rachael finished filling in the form and made several notes on her legal pad. She then turned to her computer and began dancing with her fingers across the keyboard.

Rachael chose some possibilities from the screen, made notes on some, and turned the screen so that she could show pictures of various units to Reggie. Reggie rejected some choices just from the pictures he saw and nodded and said, "Maybe," to other selections. They went at it for about thirty minutes.

Soon, the printer behind Rachael started ejecting color prints of what he assumed were possible rentals for him. He was amazed at the number..."And they said it would be difficult to get a place," he thought to himself.

Rachael spun in her chair and retrieved the output of the printer and separated them into two piles. She picked up the larger pile. "Here are the possibilities outside of Bethany Beach proper," she picked up the other, much smaller, pile, "And these are the possibilities in Bethany."

Reggie's shoulder's imperceptibly drooped. Now he was disappointed.

Rachael picked up on it and said, "Don't fret. We'll find you something you'll like. Come on. Let's go for a ride," she said gathering the papers and coming around her desk, "We'll take my car."

Reggie followed her down the corridor where Rachael told Tammy they were going to check out rentals and she would be available on her cell if anyone called.

"Nice to me you, Reggie," Tammy chirped as Rachael and Reggie made their way out of the office.

Rachael's four-door, pearl white, BMW was parked facing the building and she signaled for Reggie to get in. She pulled out into traffic and headed north on Route 1 and took a left on Garfield Parkway away from the beach. She drove a short way and turned into a neighborhood and handed him the first paper on the stack saying, "This is a nice place. It's a second floor, four room apartment in your price range. Here it is on the right. What do you think?"

"I was hoping for something within walking distance of the beach and this looks a bit run down." In addition to the dilapidated look, there were what seemed hundreds of kid's toys strewn all over the yard. There was also a refrigerator beside the side door...outside. This place would not be quiet and he wasn't interested in being invited to their parties.

"OK," said Rachael, "But let's look at a couple of more up this way."

They drove around a bit and some properties were nice and fit what Reggie had asked for except for the beach. Some were in Bethany but on the edge of town. Some were outside of Bethany, but Reggie was beginning to get the idea that even at the high-end of his price range, getting on the beach side of Route 1, was probably not going to be possible.

"I'll show you one more today; just so you can see what you were asking me for."

Rachael drove across Route 1 toward the beach and went about three blocks from town and two blocks from the beach. She pulled up in front of a four unit, two floor condo.

"Let's get out and look at this one." She said, "My legs are getting a bit cramped.

Reggie would not wish that those legs would suffer any hardship so he agreed and they went up the side stairs. The view going up the stairs was great and the Atlantic from the small porch looked good, too. Rachael opened the door with a pass key and held it for him. She leaned in just a little as he passed so that he had to brush against her lightly. 'She must sell a lot of houses,' he thought. Her pitch was great.

"This is about two blocks from the beach. Its three-room efficiency with most of the things you asked for."

Reggie looked around and indeed this would fit the bill. Near the beach, enough room to relax, and a small deck...he could even see the water a little. The bedroom was sufficient, a nice sitting room, and an eat-in kitchen.

"There's only one problem...it's about $1,000 per month more than you want to spend."

"That's a bit of a stretch, "he agreed, "But this would sure be great." He could definitely see himself in this unit but the price was out of the question. He wasn't getting his hopes up and was looking a bit forlorn.

"Don't give up yet. I only did a quick search of the properties under contract with us. Give me the rest of the day to search more thoroughly and I'll get back to you tomorrow. Do you have a cell number?" she asked as she was locking up and they were making their way down the stairs.

Reggie exchanged numbers with Rachael and she dropped him back at the Bethany Shores Motel. He kicked around his room for awhile and tried to kill some time by watching TV but he was too anxious. He decided to go for a ride.

He backed his car out of spot number 12, merged into the traffic, and headed north on Route 1. He had only been in town a couple of days and the traffic already seemed heavier as he drove. Reggie passed the stationary helicopter on a stick at the Delaware National Guard Training site. The Huey was still on guard over Bethany seemingly watching for trouble spots. He entered the causeway northbound he had used to get to Bethany.

Along the route, there were sighting towers. He could imagine coast-watchers scanning the horizon for enemy ships during World War II. They would stand watch for hours looking for the evidence of enemy submarines, ships, and planes waiting for the moment the Axis Powers would attempt a landing of spies or God forbid, an all out invasion. In that case, those in the sighting towers could help to aim the large guns located on shore to zero in on the ships.

The invasion never came and there have been varied stories of spies being landed along the eastern coast of the United States but the guns had only been used sporadically and been fired more for practice than at actual German ships.

Reggie came to Dewey Beach, the next town north of Bethany. Dewey had allowed more development along the waterfront so that there were tall hotels and condos between Route 1 and the shore. Reggie did not wish to go further north into Rehoboth, where he knew the traffic would be heavier, so he turned around in a parking lot and headed south along the same route.

He was a bit down from what he had seen today with Rachael. He knew she would find him something suitable but if he didn't get closer to the beach, his summer would not be what he had envisioned. The day had brought him new acquaintances: Lexie at the diner and Tammy & Rachel at the realty office. Reggie was sure he would see them again. He did not harbor much hope of finding that dream condo or apartment as he returned to the motel and slept fitfully.

Chapter 4: You've Got a Friend

Reggie found himself once again at the diner the next morning but something had happened overnight. The place was jammed and he didn't see an open seat. Lexie saw his dilemma and came over to him. She blew an errant hair from her face.

"Welcome to summer in Bethany. It's getting toward the end of June. The families are arriving and the rentals are filling up. It'll be getting busy everywhere soon. Even the parcels of sand on the beach will be getting smaller."

"Good morning to you, too, Lexie. You look a little busy today."

"Don't worry. It'll slow down soon...say after Labor Day. You might want to start coming a bit later or earlier, say after 8:00, but more tourists come then, too," she said looking around. "I have an idea though. Follow me."

Lexie started weaving through the tables and stopped at a booth near the back where a man was seated alone.

"Reggie, meet Joe Finley. Joe this is Reggie. Reggie is a retired school principal and Reggie, Joe is a retired cop from Philadelphia" she said in the way of introduction. "Do you mind Joe if Reggie joins you this morning? We seem to be a bit busy."

"Sure," answered Joe. "Have a seat, Reggie," he said as he extended a large hand in Reggie's direction as he put his newspaper aside. Joe had dark hair with gray showing at the temples. He had a large moustache but was otherwise clean shaven. He wore a short sleeve button shirt with blue swirls and a palm tree.

Reggie shook Joe's hand that easily encircled his. "Thanks," Reggie said, "I think the lunch menu would be up before I got a seat at the bar."

"Welcome to summer in Bethany."

"That's what Lexie said."

"Get here early to beat the crowd or you wait with the tourists outside the door."

Lexie returned with coffee for Reggie and refilled Joe's cup. "What do you want this morning, Reggie?"

"What is that you're eating, Joe?"

"It's SOS." injected Lexie.

"It's chipped beef on toast. We used to call it shit on a shingle in the Army, "said Joe.

"Is it any good? It looks terrible. I saw it in the Air Force and wouldn't eat it even though it was free"

"You either love it or hate it," stated Joe, "Really sticks to your ribs though," and he took another bite.

"OK, I'm feeling reckless this morning. SOS it is with a side of bacon."

"Commin' up," said Lexie, "And don't forget to double up on your Lipitor today."

Reggie noticed that the usual crowd was around the police chief at their usual table. They spoke in hushed tones but were frequently interrupted by people stopping by the table to converse with one or all of them.

"Town brain trust," said Joe. "Town council members and the police chief...they pretty much feel that they control things around here. Most have been in office for some time. The one sitting opposite the police chief is Marty McCabe. He's the town council president."

"Pretty much the same everywhere," Reggie agreed, "How long you be here, Joe?"

"Been here about four years. I retired as a detective from the Philadelphia PD. Needed something a little less exciting. What about you?"

"Retired school administrator from Rhode Island. I've been down here three times. Stayed in Rehoboth and in Ocean City but I like the vibe here better so I'm trying it until Labor Day."

"School administrator, huh? And I thought I had a dangerous job. Where are you staying?"

"It wasn't that bad, if you kept your head down. I'm staying at the Bethany Shores Motel for a week and I'm working with Blue Sky Realty to find something for the long term," said Reggie.

"Who's your agent? I hear they're pretty slick over there."

"Rachel Short..."

"Oh, yeah. Nice legs. Not hard to look at but there are more sharks on the land around here than in the water and she's one in the lead pack."

"I'll be careful."

Lexie appeared with the SOS. "Here you go. I see you two are getting along."

"We're from the same era. Not sweet, young, and wholesome like you."

"Don't I wish? I'm just a hash slingin', glamour queen supporting a 12 year old. Have a nice day boys. No hurry on the check." She refilled their coffee cups, laid down the checks, and was off seating more customers.

"See you on the beach, Lexie," quipped Joe as she walked away giving him a wink.

"Did Rachael show you anything worthwhile?" he asked turning back to Reggie.

"That nice pair of legs but not anything I really liked in the way of rentals or anything that was affordable. Where do you live, Joe?"

"I bought a condo on the other side of Route 1. My balcony overlooks the Delaware National Guard Training site. And I can see the ocean a bit."

"You're by that helicopter on the stand?"

"That's the place."

"I was hoping for something on this side of Route 1 but I don't want to break the bank," said Reggie.

"Good luck with that. Most of the primo property around here has been tied up by old money for generations. Property passes from generation to generation. It's tough to find something to buy or even rent. You'll find something but at this late date, it might not be ideal. How do you like your SOS?"

"It's a lot better than it looks. Thanks for the recommendation."

"World's best kept secret. Learned to like it in the Army...that's where I learned to be a cop, too."

Reggie's phone buzzed in his pocket. He took it out. "Excuse me, Rachael said she would call this morning." "Hello," he said into the phone." He listened for a moment and then said, "I'll see you in ten minutes."

"Sorry. That was Rachael," Reggie said to Joe. "She says she has something of a surprise for me to look at this morning...a condo rental on this side of Route 1 she thinks I'll like. I hope it's not over my head"

"Well things move pretty fast in the realty business around here. I've got to get going anyway. I do a little part-time work. Are you coming here tomorrow?"

"Probably for dinner and tomorrow morning."

"I guess I'll see you then. Good luck with the condo and watch out for the sharks."

"Sure thing, thanks. See you tomorrow and thanks for the seat."

Joe slid from the booth and said a few hellos as he made his way out the door. Reggie finished his breakfast, which he found rather good and prayed his arteries didn't explode in the next few hours. He paid the check and made his way to the door. He was standing in front of the diner as the white BMW approached. True to her word, Rachael glided to a stop in front of the diner and Reggie got in.

"Good morning," Rachael chirped, "Have I got a surprise for you!"

"The Beach Boys are coming to play in Bethany for the 4th of July parade."

"Are they still alive? No, better. I think I found you the perfect place. I got a call late yesterday from a couple. I've been handling their property for years. They rent up until June and after Labor Day, but usually come down themselves for July and August. The husband called and said to rent the unit for July and August because they couldn't come to Bethany at all this year. It seems his wife was in poor health. I immediately thought of you and it's on the beach side of Route 1"

"How much is this going to cost?"

"Don't worry about it for now. Here we are."

They had only driven two blocks and were on the first street running parallel to the beach. This was more of what he was looking for but again...how much would it cost? They went up the side stairs to the second floor of a two-condo unit.

"The first floor is here for the summer. They are an older couple that bought the place in partnership with the couple that can't come this year. What do you think?" Rachael swept her arm as if displaying the winning prize on "The Price is Right."

She was justified in her excitement and Reggie was catching the vibe. There were four rooms: kitchen, dining, den, and bedroom with a master bath. It was done in an open style with great materials, the latest in appliances, and huge TV/Entertainment center. As he was walking around admiring what he saw, he switched the overhead light in the bedroom. It didn't come on. He tried the lamp; dead. And then he noticed that the clock/radio had no time displayed.

"I'll get my husband to fix that this afternoon, Rachael said from behind him in the doorway. He has an electrician's business in town. It's probably just a breaker."

Reggie tried a few other lights in other rooms and they worked fine. Rachael was probably right. It didn't seem like a big deal. Everything else was great: the space, the view, and deck.

"I told them about you and your top end price and they said 'Give it to him'" because they like the idea of renting all summer to a reliable tenant, which I said you were."

"Thanks. And they will accept that as a monthly rent and are utilities included and the light problem gets fixed today?" Reggie asked.

"All included and my husband will take care of it. You pay me directly and I forward the payment to the owners."

Reggie went out on to the deck that faced the ocean and the morning sun. It was fabulous...just what he had wanted. "I'll take it. When can I move in?"

"We'll go up to the office, sign some papers, and it's yours until Labor Day."

"Sounds great...and thank you. This is going to be a great summer"

And that's how Reggie got to be a resident of Bethany Beach, Delaware.

Chapter 5: Summer Breeze

That afternoon, Reggie gathered his boxes and moved out of the Bethany Shores Motel. His rent for the week was prepaid and non-refundable but he was ready to move on. Since his summer rental started immediately, he said goodbye to Larry and drove the short distance to his new place. He unpacked his suitcases, emptied his boxes, and found places for his things. There was a bureau for him to use and a closet but there were others that were secured. He supposed they belonged to the owners...things they did not want to cart back and forth from home.

He relaxed on the deck for a while. The view was great but to get compete shade in the morning he would have to sit on the west-side and there was no view of the ocean there. So he aligned a chair with the table umbrella and enjoyed the sea breeze. He enjoyed some relax time but he soon grew restless and decided to go for a ride.

This time he decided to go south toward Ocean City. He passed over Fenwick Island...a wide causeway really...and entered the tourist Mecca, four-lane, busy, take your family to the beach, all you can eat snow crab capital of Ocean City. He could see the Ferris wheel in the distance that was out on the pier as he plied the stop and go traffic.

The restaurants, hotels, mini-golf, arcades, and pizza parlors all beckoned the tourists to come on in...its air conditioned inside. The boardwalk started miles up the road from the pier and was all laid out according to plan. Actually it was a good plan.

Next to the beach was a concrete boardwalk. This incorporated a bike path and a walkway; it was so wide. The condos and hotels were inside this walkway protecting them somewhat from severe storms. There was an amusement pier at one end of the beach. This was the location of the Ferris wheel Reggie had seen from a distance. The view from the top of the wheel was spectacular, especially at night, displaying the entire Delmarva (Delaware/Maryland/Virginia) peninsula.

But Ocean City was made for families with children and thrill seekers. There was plenty to keep everybody busy here. The beach was as beautiful as Bethany, but more commercialized. Reggie visited when he wanted some night life or an all you can eat seafood buffet. Over the last few years he mostly stuck to Bethany. Quieter Bethany Beach was more his speed now.

Reggie drove back to Bethany with the windows open, enjoying the evening air. No restaurants he passed appealed to him. Driving by Stan & Ollie's, there were no parking spots so he parked his car outside his new place and walked the two a half-blocks back to the diner.

Instead of walking the street route, he walked through the town parking lot and took the beach access path across from his new place and walked on the beach. There were a few people walking and running on the beach and of course there was inevitable treasure hunter wearing the large earphones and swinging his magnetic detector back and forth. He always wondered if they found anything of real value or if they did it just to keep busy. Either way, it didn't appeal to him very much.

As he walked he saw a sign posted in the dunes. "*Future Home of the New Seaside Condos*" priced from the low $400's. Nice location but a little too much for his taste and budget. The sign was obviously not new as shown by several large dents and wear on the faded paint. There was a large empty lot behind the sign and a small restaurant he had never tried called Sam's. He made a mental note to try it sometime. He continued down the beach and took the ramp up to the short boardwalk.

He walked along the boardwalk until he came to the passage under Mango's and took the stairs coming out by the book store on to the bandstand patio. He cut diagonally across the patio and made his way past Grotto's pizza to Stan & Ollie's.

He grabbed the handle and pulled open the door to the diner. What a transformation! There were white table cloths and china set-ups on the tables. The waitresses had shifted to black and white formal uniforms and he was greeted at the door by a receptionist. The long, blond haired girl immediately asked, "Good evening, sir. Do you have a reservation?"

"Ah, no," Reggie answered, "I didn't know I needed one."

"I'm sorry. We're all booked up. The summer season is tough. You really need to call ahead."

"Could I sit at the bar and have a drink? I see an open seat there."

"Oh, sure…you don't need a reservation for that. Also, our full menu is available at the bar," she said sweeping her arm as to invite him to pass.

Reggie started walking toward the now fully functional bar. The liquor rack had been uncovered and other patrons were sitting at the bar engaged in conversation. Some were eating dinner. Before he got there, however; he was confronted by Lexie.

"Welcome to the dinner crowd. Can't find a place to sit?"

"I was just going to sit at the bar and have dinner there."

"Suit yourself. Did you notice Joe is sitting back there?" Reggie followed her finger and there was Joe sitting with another gray-haired man with his back to Reggie. Joe was waving him back. Reggie returned the wave, thanked Lexie, and made his way to the booth.

"Hi, Joe. It really gets busy in here for dinner and the place looks great."

"Welcome again to summer in Bethany. This is Lamar Stanton, our local police chief. Lamar, this is Reggie Slater, retired school principal from Rhode Island."

Reggie turned to the gray-haired gentleman who was now extending his hand.

"I didn't recognize you out of uniform, Chief. Nice to meet you," Reggie said shaking the Chief's hand. The Chief was wearing an open collared short-sleeve white shirt and gray slacks. He somehow looked smaller out of uniform.

"Lamar is fine when I'm out of uniform."

"And Reggie suits me fine, Lamar." Reggie took a seat facing Joe and next to Chief Slater.

"How was your day, Joe?" Reggie asked.

"Not too hectic. It was kind of chores day. Shopping, cleaning up, running errands, and not much more than that. How about you?"

"Rachael found me a great place one block from the beach." Reggie told the story of his new place and where it was to both Joe and Lamar. He was still excited about it.

"I know the place," said Lamar "and the owners too. The Redmond's are great people. His brother and sister-in-law live downstairs. They're nice, too. That's a great spot for the summer. You were lucky to get it."

"Don't I know it after looking at places the day before? This place really fits the bill. And how was your day Chief...err...Lamar. Can't be too busy for you here compared to the state police?"

"Well it's busier than you think...especially in the summer. With so many people living so close together you're bound to have some conflicts, loud parties and such. And the kids, well they do what kids do, especially on the beach.

"I guess you're busier than I thought," Reggie commented.

"It keeps me busy enough, but I rest up in the winters and its better than the rat race I came from. I was with the Delaware state police before this gig and there was enough politics for me there to last a lifetime. It's this guy," Lamar pointed at Joe. "That guy gives me fits sometimes."

"Who me, what do I do?" Joe said defending himself a mock hurt look on his face.

"You and that lawyer friend of yours poking into other people's business all the time," said Lamar kiddingly pointing an accusing finger at Joe.

"Hey, I just find out the truth...people make their own problems," Joe defended himself raising his hands as if to shield himself. "I just work enough to keep me off the street."

"You're right about people making their own problems, but you don't always have to find out the whole truth."

"Hey, that's what they pay me for."

It was a pleasant dinner and Reggie was happy to have met another member of the Bethany community. Afterwards he strolled through town and back to his place. He perched on his deck with a book and a glass of wine and enjoyed the evening.

He saw people perched on their own porches enjoying coffee or reading. There were couples snuggled in beach chairs sipping wine. He could see people casually walking the beach; some alone others in couples holding hands. The town seemed to have a rhythm and Reggie felt himself beginning to vibrate in harmony.

Chapter 6: Smokin' in the Boy's Room

"Good morning, Joe," Reggie said as he slipped into their usual booth. He was feeling great this morning. He had slept well and was feeling good about his situation. He had checked on his place in Rhode Island. His nephew, James, had confirmed that everything was fine. He felt he didn't have to worry about that anymore. He felt James was trustworthy and would care for the place as if it was his own.

"Good morning, Reggie. How was it sleeping at your new place?"

"It felt great. There was a problem with some of the electrical yesterday but Rachael's husband took care of it and everything seems to be working fine. The place is perfect, just what I wanted and at the right price."

"Rachael was OK? No funny business?"

"Actually, she was great. She got me a good deal, I think."

"Well, you can be sure she got her commission, but if it was in line with what you were willing to pay, it seems like a great location and will be a great place to spend the summer. She's not hard to look at while you're conducting business either."

"Yes, I'm happy with it and you're right about the view. Good morning, Lexie," Reggie turned toward the usual bright smile that had appeared at the table. Joe just had coffee in front of him so Reggie figured he had already ordered.

"I'll have the two eggs scrambled with the coffee," Reggie said smiling at Lexie and reaching for the cream to put in the coffee she already had poured for him.

"I'll have mine over easy," said Joe.

"Oh. Sorry. I thought you had already ordered."

"No, I just got here. I had to make an early stop this morning."

"I'll put those orders right in," said Lexie and turned and went.

"Remember yesterday, the Chief said I did some detective work."

"I remember."

"Well, I work part-time for this lawyer in town. Usually it's just finding out if some witness or other is telling the truth so he doesn't look like a fool in court. I like it because it fills a couple of days a week. One can only have so much fun and relaxation. Anyway, the lawyer's name is Craig L'Engle. This morning he wanted to see me on a more personal matter and I wondered if you would be willing to help me out."

"Me? I don't know anything about doing detective work other than breaking up a mean girl gang or finding out if the student's dog really did eat his homework?"

"Don't worry about it. You know more than you think. Mostly it's just observation and note taking. Once I find out what Mr. L'Engle wants to know, I write up a report or just tell him depending on the case. Mostly, the observation part gets boring and I could use the company and I figured this would be right up your alley because it involves his son, a high school student. Are you interested?"

"I'd be happy to help. That sounds interesting. What do I have to do?"

Lexie delivered breakfast. "What are you boys up to today?"

"We're off fighting crime and making the streets of Bethany safe for beautiful women like you."

"You're such a flatterer, Joe. You two superheroes have a good day."

As they ate, Joe explained what Reggie's involvement would be.

"Well, that doesn't seem too hard. I'd be happy to help out. As long as you don't think I'd just be in the way."

"Nah. We can double team this and get it done quickly. Craig is really concerned that his son is into something dark."

Reggie and Joe finished up breakfast and got in Joe's car which was parked in front of Stan & Ollie's.

"I got lucky. Someone was pulling out as I pulled up or I never would have got a spot. Craig tells me his son, Patrick, is hanging around with the wrong crowd...Goths or something...and he thinks he's headed down the wrong path...he's afraid he might even be using drugs. There's a good amount of that around the local high school and the kids sure have the cash to buy what they want. The Chief has been telling me he's been having a lot of incidents there."

"Well, schools are usually slow to react unless something happens. It's good for Mr. L'Engle to be concerned. Do you have a plan?"

"Craig says his son often gives him the excuse of going to the library. He thinks it starts there but he doesn't know what else happens. His son told him he's going to the library today after class. He's in a make-up summer class for Algebra II. It gets out at 10:00AM. The library opens at 9:00. I thought it might be good if we were there when the son got there a little after 10:00."

"Well its 9:30 so we'll be right on time," said Reggie and they went up Garfield Parkway, across Route 1, and headed for the town library. The library was a modern brick structure not far off the parkway. They entered the double doors leading into a corridor with activity rooms on either side. There were posters on the walls advertising reading clubs, quilting clubs, writing clubs, and story hours for young children. As they entered the book section there were racks of books off to the left and a central area with study rooms.

Reggie got a book from one of the racks and Joe got the local newspaper. They took up positions where they could see the main entrance door. They didn't know where Patrick L'Engle would go but they knew he had to come through those doors. Wherever he went, either Joe or Reggie would be able to see him and whoever he met.

At about 10:15 Joe made a gesture indicating a young man with brown hair, clear skin, carrying a book satchel that had just entered the area. Reggie surmised that this was Patrick. He looked like a clean cut young man wearing a "Colorado State" t-shirt and shorts.

Patrick headed for one of the study rooms in the center of the library. There were windows all around the rooms so the occupants could be observed from several places in the library including the spots Reggie and Joe had chosen. The windows did not supply a complete view. People could be seen sitting at tables. You could see the people and the tables but not below the level of the table.

Patrick entered a room that was already occupied by another boy about the same age. The boy had a black leather jacket with silver chains. He had black greasy hair that seemed chopped. He also had a large earring in one ear and a stud in his eyebrow. The boys exchanged greetings and Patrick sat at the table with the Goth. They talked for a bit and Patrick reached into his pocket, counted some money, and gave it to the Goth. It was quick and Reggie couldn't observe it all because of the windows and the half walls.

The boys then touched fists and then they both left. Joe followed them outside and Reggie followed Joe after putting the book back on the shelf. The Goth walked into the local neighborhood and Patrick got into his car and left in the opposite direction.

"What do you make of that?" Reggie asked Joe scratching his head.

"Craig's right to be suspicious. I saw the money pass but I didn't see what Goth boy passed back to Patrick, if anything."

"I didn't either. What are you going to tell Mr. L'Engle?" Reggie inquired.

"Nothing, yet. I don't think we really have anything solid. Did you see more?" Joe asked.

"No. I guess I can't say what I saw except some money changed hands but I couldn't tell you why."

"So I guess that's a wrap for today but I have a problem for tomorrow. Could you do me a favor?"

"What can I do?" asked Reggie.

"I'm in court to testify for one of Craig's cases tomorrow. Could you come to the library and observe Patrick and see if you can find out any more?"

"Sure. I can do that. Today didn't take long at all and I enjoy libraries."

Reggie went back into the building, got a library card, and checked out the book he had been pretending to read. Joe gave him a ride home. "Would you like to see the place?"

"Sure," said Joe.

Joe stayed for awhile and they had coffee on the deck. Joe said he had some things to do and would meet Reggie at the diner the following morning.

Reggie took a beach chair and umbrella to the beach and passed away the afternoon basking in the sun and reading. He listened to the surf and went in the water once even though it was still a bit chilly. He moved his chair to the shallows and passed the time reading about half of the book he had checked out of the library. This was life at the beach.

"No shirt, no shoes, no problem..." he thought to himself.

Chapter 7: Be True to Your School

Reggie awoke with a start...looking around and wondering where he was for a second. Oh, yeah. He had a new place, some new friends, and something to occupy his time. So far, it was working out OK. Last week he was alone in a place he loved and now...well, it was better and his soul seemed more at peace. What was all that stress he used to carry? It was fading fast and he liked it.

In his former life, the stress never left. It followed him home. It followed him on vacation. It followed him to sleep disturbing even the peace of his dreams. Now, that burden had been lifted. He slept dream free and his mind was clear during the day. At times he felt so light like he could walk on air.

He walked to the diner for breakfast. It must have been Lexie's day off and Joe had court so he must have left earlier. He found a seat at the bar and ordered. Reggie ate quickly and waved to Chief Stanton on the way out. He was a bit anxious to get to the library, but it was too early so he decided to walk the beach for awhile. He walked through the band stand area and took the ramp over the dunes.

The tide was out so the beach was wide this morning. Reggie removed his sandals that along with shorts and a t-shirt had become his standard, daily attire. He walked down on the cool sand. He was wearing shorts so he let the waves lap at his ankles. The plovers and sand pipers played at the edges of the waves looking for morsels to eat and the gulls cried from above and on the beach...they had cleaned the beach of food and now couldn't find any human deposits to eat. The pelicans were making out better as they dived on schools of fish off shore and the ever-present dolphins patrolled about 50 feet from where he was walking. A Day in the Life...great.

As he left the beach and was at the head of the walkway that led to his place, Reggie again noticed the sign for the Seaside Condo development. It seemed that it had been erected some time ago. These developments usually went pretty quick and it seemed that this one was lingering. Maybe the project became a victim of the economic downturn and would never be built. He had seen some of those down in Florida. Some were even left partially completed as the bank funding dried up and so did the buyers.

He made his way along the path and through the small public parking lot. As he was about to cross the street, he saw a patrol car approaching and Chief Stanton pulled to the curb.

"Good morning, Reggie."

"Mornin' Chief."

"How's the beach this morning?"

"All is calm...hey, what's with the Seaside Condo development? The sign seems a bit worn? Is the project dead?"

"Oh, it's not dead. That development has been a bone of contention around here for some time. Of course the developers are anxious to build, but the town council rejected it. Seems there's some wetlands problem with a small piece of the land and Sam's Restaurant over there stands in the way. Sam's is owned by one of the town council members...the council president in fact...it's a real mess."

"Sounds like a political gaggle to me."

"You don't know the half of it. Got to get going...enjoy your day."

"You too, Chief." And he drove off. Reggie made his way back to his place and killed another hour finishing up his book.

The library wasn't too busy. He returned his book and was perusing the new release shelves when Patrick entered and went to the room he was in yesterday. He took books from his satchel and began working on something that looked like homework. Reggie could see a bit better than yesterday because he was standing. He selected a new book and picked up the local paper and went to the empty room next to the one Peter occupied. On the way, he passed close to Patrick's window and could tell he was working on algebra...must be his homework from his summer class.

About ten minutes later, Goth guy came strolling in with silver chains jingling and dressed in the same clothes as the day before. He sat down next to Patrick and they began to talk. Soon, Goth guy was writing on Patrick's homework and the pad of paper passed back and forth for over an hour. They were doing math homework! The Goth guy was tutoring Peter with his math and he seemed pretty good at it. There wasn't any drug dealing going on...the Goth guy must be a math wizard and he was tutoring Patrick.

The boys finished up their work for the day and some cash changed hands. Goth guy left and Patrick worked for awhile longer. Once he was finished, Patrick left also. Joe would be surprised...and Patrick's Dad would be relieved. He wondered why Patrick's Dad didn't know about the tutoring. Reggie checked out his new book and headed home.

That evening, he was eating dinner with Joe and told him what he had observed. Joe said that was a better outcome than he expected but he would check it out further with someone he knew at the high school just to be sure.

---***---

The next morning Joe told Reggie that he had called a teacher he knew at the high school. The teacher said he would get back to him this morning after checking the summer school roster. As they were finishing breakfast, Joe's phone rang. He talked for a few minutes and then hung up.

"Well, I guess you were right. ~~Peter~~ Patrick is taking a summer Algebra II make up class because he got a "D" last term. Jim, the teacher, knows the Goth guy and he is a math whiz and a good kid, if a bit weird with his style."

"How about that? I bet his Dad will be thrilled...well...maybe not. Seems he didn't know about the tutoring."

"I guess he'll be a little bit of both. He'll be pleased his son is not into drugs and a little concerned he is hiding the math tutor from him. Hey, why don't you come and meet Craig and we'll tell him what we found out."

"Err...OK...when?"

"Let's finish up breakfast and go to his office. I need to talk to him about developments in the case from yesterday anyway."

"Alright, if you're sure he won't mind."

"It'll be fine. Come on. Let's go."

They used Joe's car to go to Craig L'Engle's office which ironically was up near the library. It was a small office located in a wing built off a house set back off a main road. Apparently, Craig and his family lived in the attached dwelling.

"Good morning, Lucy. You're looking fine this morning." Joe was addressing the good looking secretary in the outer office. She was dressed in a red blouse and a gray skirt. They both were tasteful for the workplace but let it be known she had a good looking body underneath. She had shoulder length soft blond hair. She wore a small chain around her neck and there was no evidence of a wedding band.

"Flattery will get you everywhere. He's in and who's your friend?"

"Lucy this is Reggie...Reggie, Lucy."

"Nice to meet you, Reggie. You're not hanging around with this crass loser are you?"

"Good to meet you, too, Lucy. I'll try not to have it rub off."

"She's always so pleasant, but she really loves me. Let's go."

"With all my heart and you know it," Lucy echoed as they went down the hall and into a well appointed office.

"Good morning, Joe"

"Good morning, Craig. This is Reggie. He helped me out observing Patrick's activities."

"Oh?" Craig gave Joe and Reggie a questioning look.

Joe told Craig about the two days of surveillance and his contact with the high school teacher. The lawyer looked concerned and confused as they predicted.

"I'm thrilled he's not into something bad, but why would he lie to me about the tutor?"

Reggie chimed in, "Well, I was a principal in my former life and maybe he just didn't want to disappoint you. Kids want to please their parents so maybe he was afraid you would think less of him."

"Since his Mom died a couple of years ago it has just been the two of us and he has been a bit distant. I think Patrick and I have to have a talk. Thank you both for what you did. I really am relieved. Nice to meet you, Reggie. And thanks for helping out." Mr. L'Engle stood and offered Reggie his hand from behind his desk. "Could you give Joe and me few minutes?"

Reggie went out and made small talk with the secretary while Joe consulted with Craig. Shortly, Joe emerged from the office and they went out to Joe's car.

"Here's your cut," Joe said handing Reggie a few bills.

"I didn't do much and it was your job, not mine."

"Just the same you helped me out. Craig seems to be getting a few more cases lately and I really like the company. Would you mind doing some more detective work?"

"Sure. It was interesting and not too difficult. I wouldn't mind helping out once in a while."

"What are you doing tomorrow?"

Chapter 8: Oops! There it is.

Reggie walked to the diner in the next morning and slid into the booth opposite Joe. He had again slept well and was feeling good about the day.

"How are you today?"

"Just great," said Joe. "Are you ready for something a little more serious than yesterday?"

"What do you mean by more serious?" Reggie asked as Lexie came to take their order.

After they ordered Lexie asked, "How did the superhero crime fighters make out yesterday?"

"Reggie here is going to make detective first-grade before you know it."

"Does he get to wear the Batman suit?"

"No, he'll still be Robin for awhile. Now, go get our breakfast. I thought I just saw the Bat signal in the sky. Gotham needs us."

Lexie scurried off and Joe got serious.

"This case we have today is pretty typical of what happens around here. I've worked several like it. Families tend to own most of the beach cottages. They are used mostly by thirty to forty-something's because they are the ones that can afford it. Their kids are either real young in which case they spend all day with Mom; or teenagers meaning the kids go off on their own and Mom is alone except on the weekend. On the weekend Dad comes to visit. During the week, that leaves Mom alone and…"

"And what?" Reggie probed.

When Mom's are alone and Dad's away, some of them need to know if they're desirable anymore."

"And…"

"Do I have to spell it out for you? That means they need sexual comfort and are attracted to tennis instructors, surfing instructors, usually younger men that make them feel needed and young again."

"What do you try to do…catch them in the act?"

"I'm not a voyeur and catching them in the act is harder than you think but you need some hard evidence. Sorry about the poor choice of words. Pictures of the man or her walking into the place they meet say or them walking in or out together…holding hands or kissing. Pictures of them in the act really seal the deal but they're difficult to get," Joe explained. "So today we have the classic case of prove that I'm right or prove that I'm wrong….according to the husband"

Lexie delivered their meals and then Reggie asked, "And that is…"

"We watch until we get evidence or until the guy believes his wife and he stops paying us. If a husband is suspicious, he is also jealous but he's only jealous to a certain amount of green, if you know what I mean."

They finished up at the diner and again took Joe's car. The duo went into a neighborhood on the other side of Route 1 and South of Garfield Parkway. They found a spot on the street behind another car and slid in behind it.

"That's the house...the blue one over there."

"Nice place," Reggie remarked.

"Sure...Daddy makes plenty and keeps them all happy. There is a 15 year old daughter and Mom. Of course, Dad works in Philadelphia during the week and only comes on weekends...sometimes Thursday nights. There she is now with the daughter getting into the car." A shapely woman got into the car along with a young girl. The girl was dressed for the beach and carried a large bag.

They followed at a distance as Mom and daughter headed toward Bethany and the beach. As they left the neighborhood, Joe suddenly made a U-turn.

"Where are we going? I thought we were going to follow them."

"We will next time but for now I've got to do something. I think she is going to drop the daughter at the beach. I'll take this opportunity to get something done."

Joe parked the car where it was, got out, and went to the trunk. He took some equipment from the trunk and came around to the passenger window.

"I'll be right back."

Reggie watched as Joe approached each front door and put a leaflet on it. He proceeded on to the blue house, put the leaflet on the front door and went around the back. He emerged on the other side of the house and went to the next three houses and then returned to the car.

"What was that you were putting on the doors?"

"A flyer I picked up at the library for book clubs."

"Why did you go around back of the blue house?"

"I put a listening device on the bedroom window," Joe explained. He then showed Reggie the receiver, a small box with a recording device and a speaker. This is the microphone like the one I just put on the window." Joe showed Reggie a small device attached to a suction cup with a small antenna.

"I have several of the microphones but only one of these receiver/recorders. We can hear everything that goes on in that room with this." Joe also showed Reggie a camera with a telephoto lens.

"You're regular CIA."

"Nah. They have the good shit."

The woman returned shortly, parked in the driveway, and entered the house. She took the flyer from the front door and stuffed it into her pocketbook.

"See. If someone says they saw me in the neighborhood, the flyer gives me a reason and no one will think anything about it."

"You are good Batman."

They watched all day. They heard game shows, soaps and half-dozen talk shows. Nothing of interest happened.

"This is where you earn your money. Not too exciting, huh?"

"Not very. Take me home. I have a couple of steaks in the freezer and a fresh six-pack. Want to join me?" Reggie asked.

"Sounds good to me," Joe said as he drove back to Reggie's apartment.

It sounded good to Reggie, too. He hoped tomorrow would bring something better than today.

---***---

They were back at it the next day. The woman and daughter got in the car about the same time of day, but this time Joe and Reggie followed.

She drove down to the end of Garfield Parkway in town and her daughter got out, got a beach chair and a bag from the trunk and headed for the surf; probably to be with her friends for the day. Mom made the loop at the end of the street and headed back up through town. If she was heading home, she would have gone across Route 1 but instead she took a left at Chief Little Owl.

"Aha, here we go," said Joe as they followed. After a few blocks, she turned into the market parking lot, parked, and went in. After about forty-five minutes, she came out pushing a loaded grocery cart, loaded the bags into the car, and drove off.

"Unless they're meeting up in the vegetable aisle, I take it that wasn't it."

"Unless the boyfriend's a cucumber, no, it wasn't," answered Joe as he followed the woman from the parking lot.

This time the woman went back home. Joe and Reggie did a turn around the block while she brought the groceries into the house and then took up a position not too far up the block.

About an hour later they were getting fidgety and itching to get a coffee when a car pulled into the driveway of the blue house. A young man dressed in shorts and polo shirt got out and went to the door and was quickly let in. Joe was snapping pictures all the way. Joe hit the record button on the device, turned up the volume on the listening device, and they waited.

They didn't have to wait long until the action started. There were lots of kissing sounds..."Your sooo sexy"...clothes being removed..."I want you now"...and such. Joe and Reggie were smiling at each other when Reggie noticed some movement down the block and nudged Joe's arm.

"Oh, shit," said Joe.

"What?"

"It's the husband."

The action was continuing in the bedroom with the noises getting louder. The husband went to the side yard where the bedroom was. Joe moved the car so they could get a clear view. The woman certainly wasn't coming to the window now.

The husband retrieved a ladder from the bushes, set it up, and peered into the bedroom window. He started banging on the window and yelling obscenities at his wife and her lover. Joe continued taking pictures. Reggie heard screams and a "What the

%#$%" over the speaker, and "What the %#@ are you doing with my wife?" yelled from the side of the house. The sex sounds suddenly stopped, a woman screamed, another man's voice said from the speaker, "Who the %#^& is that?"

The ladder was half in a flower bed and half on the lawn...and not very stable. One side started sinking into the thick mulch, the husband continued to yell, and the whole business collapsed amid screaming, swearing, name calling, and the lover running out the front door dressed only in his shorts and carrying his sandals and polo shirt, getting in his car and speeding away. Joe got more pictures.

After the boyfriend disappeared around the bend, Joe was out of the car in a flash followed by Reggie both suppressing snickers and laughter. The husband was tangled in the flower bed still fuming and struggling to get up. Joe helped him to his feet from under the ladder which had fallen on top of him. He was holding his arm saying, "I think I broke it." He was covered with dirt and plant remains.

Soon there were police and EMT's on the scene. The man was taken to the hospital for treatment...yelling at his wife until the Rescue Truck door's closed. The wife could be heard yelling and sobbing from the living room with the front door open. Joe had quietly retrieved the microphone from the bedroom window and put it in his pocket figuring this was the end of the job.

Reggie, Joe, and Chief Stanton stood on the front lawn with neighbors peering from their windows up and down the street.

"This is like the old joke of setting off the fire alarm in a student dorm...then you know who's sleeping with whom," the

Chief quipped shaking his head, "What a scene; another nice job boys. I think your work here is done."

Joe and Reggie got into their car and halfway out of the neighborhood burst out laughing.

Chapter 9: Baby You Can Drive My Car

Marty McCabe had had a particularly difficult day. First, at the diner during breakfast the realty group had harassed him. That Seaside Condo issue just would not die. Before that, at home his wife, Jill, was in rare form and nagging him about the restaurant again. She just thought that running the place was a waste of time and effort. She just didn't get it. But the killer was the town council meeting.

Most of the meeting had gone along as planned and then they zeroed in on those damned Seaside Condos, again. For years now it was the same arguments over and over and it just wouldn't stop. Time after time he fought, cajoled, skirted, and manipulated...and he was weary of the fight. He had won many battles, but the war was a siege and it was wearing him down. The issue of the building permits had been defeated at the federal and local level several times and each time, he thought it was over. Then, from another angle, the fight would start anew. When would it end?

He had gone from the town council meeting back to his restaurant, Sam's, to check on the dinner crowd. Tina, the hostess, said business had been a bit slow. Marty had thought business would pick up this week with the arrival of the summer crowd but it hadn't happened yet. Etienne, his chef, had been in a foul mood because of the small crowd. Marty left at about 9:00PM because he was tired. He was physically and mentally drained from the day.

The pressure to build the Seaside Condo units had ebbed and flowed over the last two years. In the beginning, it had been easy for the town council to turn it down. There was a small estuary on the property next to the parking lot that abutted his restaurant. The environmental impact study had deemed it a wildlife habitat that could not be disturbed. The issue was DOA.

But the developers would not be deterred. They came up with a plan to relocate the wildlife habitat as had been done when the town had built the bandstand and brought the matter to the Town Counsel once again with a new EPA study approving the wetlands relocation. The wetland was to be relocated to his restaurant property which they would acquire. So now he was in it up to his neck. The developers were hounding him to sell the restaurant property and he was fighting the overall issue of the development with the town council and it seemed like everybody else. His wife wanted him to sell out because of the time commitment, everyone else wanted him to sell out because of the development and the profits that it would mean for everyone.

There were many that did not support the Seaside Condo development but, it seemed that not many of those came to the meeting. He had been accused of holding back the project now because of his own restaurant and it looked like he had a conflict of interest. It wasn't that at all. Bethany had a tradition. Since the old hotels on the beach were destroyed by storms, only hotels off the beach were permitted and not many of them at that. Bethany was mostly a family town with cottages and summer homes and that was what he was fighting to protect. Why couldn't he get others to see it? This development was bad for Bethany. It would further change the character of the town.

During the last session with the environmental issue out of the way, it had been a bitter fight. The counsel was split and he, Marty McCabe the Town Council President, had cast the deciding vote, nay. And the issue was dead for another season. Oh, but not so fast, it was here again and it was worse this time. The counsel was split and so was his own house.

Jill, Marty's wife, wanted him to end the fight. "Give in," she had said. "Get rid of that restaurant and retire. Between the Town Council and the restaurant you're always working. It's eating you alive." And she was right in some respects.

Well, it wasn't as bad as she made it out to be. He had a great chef at the restaurant that had remained a constant for four years. Marty also had an enterprising manager that he paid well. This kept the restaurant management fairly honest and efficient. It also produced a tidy profit for Marty that kept Jill's appetite for the finer things satisfied. But now she wanted him to give up the restaurant and the town council. Besides, he liked being a big man on campus at his...yes, his restaurant where he could hand out tables as favors that garnished votes that kept both his pastimes satisfied. He had always been well known in town and he liked it that way. If he sold out he would probably fade into oblivion.

Marty was not originally a restaurateur nor had he ever planned to run one but circumstances had just played out that way. He was actually a pharmacist. He had owned the local pharmacy just outside of town. That had worked for 30 years and his plan was to sell the business to a young pharmacist and retire. Well, the plan didn't work as well as he had hoped.

A few years before he planned to sell, CVS moved into town and then Walgreens. CVS made him a deal he could not refuse and he took it. The money was not as much as he wanted but what else could he do. The two huge pharmacy chains were sucking him dry. So, he sold out and bought the restaurant. Turns out he was pretty good at it and enjoyed running a restaurant. And the extra money made up for what CVS shorted him on the pharmacy...and Jill didn't mind that so much.

"But no, she just can't leave it alone," he said aloud as he pulled into the liquor store parking lot. He went in and picked up a six pack of beer, some wine that Jill liked, and then went to the bourbon section to get something for himself. He liked bourbon, but usually got the reasonably priced stuff. This time he wanted some good stuff.

He picked up a rectangular bottle with a top seal. This looked good...he deserved it...Knob Creek the label read. He went to the checkout. Marty swiped his card, mindlessly punched in the code, told the clerk to have a nice day and put the bag in the back of the king cab. He backed out of the parking spot and continued down the road toward home to the small gentleman's farm on the edge of town, more in the country than at the beach.

As he rode down the straight two-lane road towards the farm, he was passing other farm fields. He started wondering about his purchases. It seemed like he paid an awful lot for that bourbon. How much was that? He turned on the cruise control and reached back into the bag. He fished around until he felt the rectangular bottle. He grabbed it by the neck and brought it into the front seat.

Marty turned the bottle around in his hand. He was looking for the price in the poor light when the truck suddenly sped up. He tried to control the truck but he caught the rut on the side of the road and the engine was screaming. He veered into the corn field and tried to lift the accelerator pedal with his foot. The corn plants were not very tall and the truck was still gaining speed. He was steering with one hand and the steering wheel was wrenched from his hand and suddenly the truck was airborne.

It all slowed down just then. He could hear the engine's high pitched whine as the wheels lost purchase. Everything was floating as if weightless. He could not feel the seat and the steering wheel did nothing when he turned it...and then everything stopped. Well, at least the truck stopped but everything else kept moving. The bottle, still in his hand headed for the dashboard and shattered spilling that expensive bourbon all over him...all over everything. Something...something large was headed right for the windshield...what was that?

The airbag in the steering wheel exploded in his face and his hands shot forward. There were things breaking all around him. And then just for a second everything was silent and the smell of the bourbon was everywhere..."My, that smells sweet," he thought...and it all stopped.

Chapter 10: You've Got a Friend

"Can you believe it? These two jokers are watching this woman and the husband shows up and breaks his arm playing peeping Tom on his own wife and nose diving into the rose bushes."

Lexie was listening intently and was now giggling. "And you got the whole thing on tape with pictures?"

"Dead to rights...pictures, audio in the act, case closed," Joe said.

"I'd love to be in that courtroom for that divorce hearing. Be tough to keep the jury under control," Reggie chimed in. "Probably wouldn't have to call too many more witnesses."

"Wouldn't know whether to convict the wife or the husband...maybe both," the Chief commented.

"Sure would be tough for me...a real dumb and dumber," Lexie decided.

"And further, these two crime fighters..." Chief Stanton was interrupted by the crackle of his radio. "This is BP1," the Chief answered into the radio.

"BP-6 & BP-7 are on the scene of that accident reported on outer Lee Road just before the McCabe place. Seems it happened overnight and was reported by a passing motorist. They would like your assistance."

"Roger...I'm responding. BP1 out," Chief Stanton responded into his radio and to the group, "Got to go."

"Mind if we tag along?" asked Joe.

"If you can stay out from under my feet and not hurt anybody."

"We'll be good," Reggie and Joe answered in unison.

"Come on, let's go. And remember, you're just observers."

They drove out to the scene without red lights and siren but at a good pace. The Chief parked on the side of the road behind the two other local police cars and two state police units. The Chief, Joe, and Reggie walked through the corn field following the tracks of a vehicle in the soft dirt. The remaining corn was about two feet high. As they approached, they could see tracks ran up to a small rise and then the tracks disappeared for about 50 feet and then reappeared right before a huge oak tree. There was a green Ford King Cab pickup imbedded in the tree. About 30 feet short of the crowded scene, the chief turned to them and said, "Stay here. Let me see what's going on."

The Chief proceeded closer to the accident scene and the local officers and the state police patrolmen gathered around him. There was a lot of pointing and hand gestures as the officers appeared to be explaining what they had found. Joe turned and looked back at the tire tracks and then turned back and looked toward the truck and the tree. Then, he started walking back toward the road following the tracks in the dirt. Reggie followed.

"What are you looking for, Joe?"

"I'm trying to picture in my mind what happened." They reached the road and Joe stared intently at the beginning of the wheel marks. "See that. The tires were stuck in that rut. See, way back there and then they turn into the field. The truck should have slowed as it went through the field, but by the impact, it doesn't seem so. Then," and they were walking toward the rise, "It hits this rise and goes airborne...see, no tracks. It comes down and slams into the tree. Must have been one hell of an impact! It almost looks like he drove it in...like he wanted it to happen."

"What do you mean?" Reggie asked.

"It just seems like the driver never slowed down."

Just then, Chief Stanton approached them. They were standing near the rise in a small circle. "This is not for publication...its Marty McCabe, the Town Council president. Seems he died instantly when he hit the tree. It happened sometime last night. A passing motorist saw it this morning. Hard to pick out, it's a bit of a distance from the road and the small rise somewhat blocks the view."

"Chief I'm looking at these tracks and..." Joe started to talk about the cause of the accident and the Chief cut him short.

"Look Joe, I don't mean to cut you off but Marty and I were good friends. I now have to go and tell his wife Jill what happened. Can we save this for later?

"Sure Chief."

They drove to the McCabe place which was only a short distance away. They went down a long, dirt driveway that led to a circular asphalt drive in front of the house. There was a barn and a large shed on the property. The house was typical of a farm with a large wraparound porch.

Joe and Reggie waited in the patrol car and Chief Stanton climbed the front stairs to the porch and went into the house to see

Mrs. McCabe. When he came out twenty minutes later, Lamar Stanton looked pretty distraught.

"She took it hard," he said. "She was just now looking for him and thought he was out in the barn or something. She went to bed early last night and took something to help her sleep. She didn't even know he was missing...never mind dead."

Chief Stanton dropped Reggie and Joe off and then returned to the scene. Lamar could see the tow truck from the local garage hooking up the truck and pulling it away from the tree as he walked from the road. The driver was checking the hook up as the Chief approached his officers that were congregated off to the side.

"Where do we stand?" the Chief asked.

The patrolman answered, "Mr. McCabe has been taken to the local morgue. The State Police were cooperative and understanding after you talked to them. The truck is being towed to the impound yard at the town garage. No doubt about what happened, huh?"

"The truck reeks of booze but Mrs. McCabe doesn't need to know that. He was going too fast, lost control, and hit a tree. He's dead. That's bad enough."

"Right, Chief. We protect our own."

"Damn straight."

---***---

The following morning Joe, Reggie, and Chief Stanton were at their regular booth. Joe was explaining what he had observed at the scene and the Chief listened intently.

"...so, if I had to guess I would say that he drove that thing right off the road. Once he hit the rise, he was out of control and the rest is what we saw this morning," Joe concluded.

"Does any of that speculation change the outcome or does it just cause the family more pain?" asked the Chief.

"Mostly more pain."

"So, if we just say some of the facts instead of all the facts and add your speculation we have Marty McCabe driving too fast in the dark, losing control of his car, hitting a tree and dying instantly. If we leave out the booze and the other thoughts you've said, we still have what we can prove minus the booze and he's still dead. It doesn't affect anybody else, does it? It surely doesn't affect the outcome," the Chief added.

"No it doesn't...I see your point," said Joe.

"So, let's just leave it be and put him to rest at his funeral. He served the town well and was respected. Let it be."

"OK, Chief. I see what you mean."

"You, too?" the Chief turned to Reggie, "We don't mention it again...to anyone."

"OK," said Reggie.

"OK what," asked Lexie as she appeared at their table.

"OK we're going to Marty McCabe's funeral on Tuesday," said Joe.

"They were talking about that over there, too," Lexie said.

"Where, Lexie?"

"The Town Council guys and Rachael Short," Lexie answered.

Turning to look, they saw the council members seated at their regular table with Rachael Short. They seemed to be listening to Rachael and then nodding their approval about something. They were obviously in agreement with whatever she was saying.

"Rachael Short," said the Chief turning toward their table, "What else is she talking to them about?" asked the Chief.

"Well, I wasn't eves dropping or anything but Chris Donnelly is talking about appointing someone to finish Marty's term on the council. Chris is the vice-president of the Council and probably will be elected president so he should know the procedures. Rachael put her husband, Alan, up for the job and is trying to convince them that he's the right man for the appointment."

"You mean 'We Fix Your Shorts' Alan Short?" asked Joe.

"He fixed the electrical problem in my apartment," added Joe.

"What makes him qualified to serve on the Town Council?" asked the Chief.

"He's as qualified as any of them. They're all just businessmen in the community," Lexie said gesturing toward their table.

They all nodded in agreement.

"There's only five months left to go on Marty's term so they can probably appoint rather than hold a special election," stated Chief Stanton, "Sounds right. I'm sure they know the rules. There's no moss on Rachael though. She shows up the day after Marty's accident and puts her husband up for his seat. It's almost like she planned it."

They finished their dinners and Reggie declined a ride home and walked the beach. The sand was cool on his bare feet but the water was pleasantly warm from the day's sun. There were several stars out and a crescent of a moon. It was a pleasant night with soft surf providing a soothing background. There was some lightning out over the water in the darkness of the sliver of a moon. Funny though, there was no thunder.

Chapter 11: Surf City

Reggie was a bit weary of all of the excitement lately and decided to take a day for himself. He ate breakfast with Joe at the diner and then headed south for Ocean City. Reggie thought he would find some distractions in Ocean city because it was Saturday and Joe was busy finishing up a case with Craig. The traffic would be a bit heavy because of the weekend but he could stand to be around some families and rub shoulders with people having fun for awhile. The last few days had been a bit of a drag with talk of Marty McCabe's accident dominating the minds of all the people of Bethany. His death had cast a pall over the town and interrupted the usual summer excitement, at least for town residents.

The day started bright and beautiful but the Weather Channel was predicting some possible afternoon showers. Right now though he had all the windows open in the car and the ocean breeze was blowing through. Reggie, luckily, found a parking spot a block from the beach and walked through to the boardwalk. He began to walk north and stopped to watch a street performer. The tall buildings facing the beach made Reggie look up. The hotels or condos, he didn't know which nor could he tell one from the other, loomed large over the boardwalk and would cast a large afternoon shadow over the beach. For now though, the beach was in the bright sunlight.

The young man with a coarse beard was playing an acoustic guitar and singing some Bon Jovi tunes. He sang about Tommy working on the docks and his girlfriend Gina toiling away in the diner...and their dreams of a life together. He had a surprisingly good voice. The guitarist shifted to Bryan Adams and that song in the Chevy commercials. He was a talented performer and here he was playing for change in Ocean City. Reggie threw a five-dollar bill in the guitar case and thanked him. "He stuffed the bill in his shirt," Reggie thought as he walked on.

Reggie walked south for awhile. There were many people on the beach and they seemed to be having a fine day. There was a group playing volley ball at the public nets. They were young and sweaty and were high-fiving each other when they made a point. He wondered how many knew each other before the game and how many new friends there would be after the game was over. The colleges were out and many sons and daughters had moved to Daddy's condo on the beach. Most of them had jobs in the restaurants and tourist attractions that would not begin until later in the day. For now they were free to play on the beach and life was good.

Reggie walked on to the amusement pier. There were the usual carnival barkers enticing the tourists to play the games and win their wives, girlfriends, or children a big stuffed animal. "Three balls for a dollar! Three chances to win," they shouted at the passers-by. The crowds were thin this early in the day and there were few takers. Continuing down the pier, Reggie came to the Ferris wheel. "Why not?" he thought to himself and bought a ticket.

He waited in the short line as the wheel loaded and finally he was seated in the chair. The chair rocked and Reggie held on as the wheel rotated. Up and up he moved as other chairs were loaded below him. The noise of the pier subsided as he rose and the crowd grew smaller and smaller until he was at the top looking back toward Bethany across Fenwick Island; alone at the top with his thoughts. It was a bit disconcerting to be surrounded by nothing but air. His balance played tricks with his mind and he felt himself gripping the bar tighter.

He had made some new friends since coming to Bethany. He was pleased with that. There was Lexie at the diner and Chief Stanton. There was Joe and his lawyer friend, Mr. L'Engle, that filled some of his time. There were other town officials that he was coming to know more about...and the more he learned about them the more they seemed a lot like the people he knew back in Rhode Island. The faces and names were changed but much about politics and the interaction of people was the same. Reggie had never made friends easily being the quiet man he was, but he had made an effort and he was pleased with the results. He was becoming more of a resident and less of a tourist.

It was a stroke of luck that he had landed an apartment near the beach for the summer. It was peaceful there with a nice deck and he had his books and his crossword puzzles. His days were full and yet there was something nagging at ....the wheel began to move and he went round and round...he lost count of how many times. He had to smile like a kid as the world rotated before his eyes and he alternately felt that sinking and rising feeling in his gut.

As he rose and fell, he could see Bethany, Fenwick, Ocean City, the ocean, the boats...it was all so beautiful...it was all so peaceful. This retirement business was fun. The wheel unloaded car by car as it had loaded and he came to a stop at the top once more rocking back and forth in his seat. All and all it had been a good start to the summer and he did like the people he had met. He could make a life here...hey, it was better than being buried in snow in Rhode Island. He wondered how much snow they got in Delaware in the winter time.

After his Ferris wheel ride, Reggie walked off of the pier and entered a small restaurant and took a seat at the bar. He ordered a beer and a sandwich and watched the Nationals game on TV.

Maybe he should watch more baseball. It seemed relaxing. And the beer was good, too. He stayed for a couple of innings nursing his beer. Then he slowly walked back to his car and drove back toward Bethany.

When he got home, he found a note taped to his door. It read, "See me tomorrow AM at the diner," it was signed "Joe."

Chapter 12: Will You Still Love Me Tomorrow

"Good morning, Joe,"

"Good morning. Reggie" They were alone in the booth this morning. As usual, Lexie poured their coffee and took their order.

"What's with the note on my door?"

"It's nothing for today, it's for tomorrow but I wanted to talk to you about it first. This new case has to be a bit quieter and confidential. One of the town council members asked Craig L'Engle to look in on his wife's activities and to be very tight lipped about it. He's wondering what she's up to. He doesn't necessarily believe she's cheating on him but he thinks she might be involved in some shady business dealings. He's a bit of a nervous Nellie and seems spooked by his own shadow but this is a bit different for me, too."

"How so?"

"Well, most of the divorce cases I help out with are like what you saw last week. Husband out of town...wife fools around or sometimes the other way around. They don't all divorce, even if we get the evidence, because it's too expensive but the husband pays the price in different ways but anyway one of the parties is usually out of town. Mr. and Mrs. Leeman both live here in Bethany. He's not accusing her of cheating but thinks she may be up to no good with her friends and he just wants some insight as to what it might be she's into."

"That's a bit of an odd and open-ended request. It doesn't seem to end with any kind of prosecution for wrong doing or a crime so why is Craig involved?"

Lexie brought their meals and refilled their coffee. "How are you today Reggie?"

"Good, Lexie, but the whole town seems a bit down," Reggie observed.

"Probably be that way until after the funeral," and she left to continue pouring more coffee and tend to other customers.

"To answer your question, it seems they're old friends and this is a favor. So, we'll need to be more subtle. Change cars, change surveillance times, and be coyer all-around so we're not spotted. You in?"

"Sure but can we cut back to half days...I need some beach time."

"Sounds good to me, too. We can't watch all day anyway...we'd probably get spotted. We'll have to do some asking around to gather information, too. And it would be better if we go about this slowly so as not to attract any attention so half-days are good."

"Alright, I'm in. Mostly to keep you company."

"Good morning, Joe. Who's your friend," said a large burly man in an apron now standing at the head of the booth. He had curly red hair, arms like a sailor, and showed his teeth when he smiled.

"Good morning, Stan. This is Reggie. Reggie this is Stan, half-owner of Stan and Ollie's."

Reggie had been wrong. Stan wasn't burly, he was a grizzly bear. His big paw reached out and encircled Reggie's hand, "There really is a Stan. I don't suppose there's also an Ollie?"

"You bet," Stan said crushing Reggie's hand and then releasing his now numb fingers. Stan turned and stuck his head in the kitchen. Another smaller, slimmer man emerged and stood beside Stan.

"This is Ollie," said Stan, "Meet Reggie."

"Anyone brave enough to sit with this guy is alright with me. Hi, Joe. Good to meet you Reggie," and Ollie shook Reggie's hand. Ollie was much smaller with black hair, a thin nose, and a dimple in his chin.

"Your real names? Stan and Ollie?" inquired Reggie.

"Stan Lighter and Ollie Needham," stated Stan. We have been friends for twenty-five years. We met right here in Bethany. As teenagers, we used to come here with our families every summer. We hung out in town and on the beach. We even had college summer jobs here."

"Stan and I went off to college," continued Ollie. "We even roomed together. I earned a culinary degree. I kicked around a few restaurants but I had always dreamed of opening a place here in Bethany."

"I went into business...got an MBA," said Stan. "That got me nowhere in the poor economy. I was making more money tending bar than working my full time job. Then Ollie called me."

"Yep. Called him out of the blue and offered to take all I had and sink it in a restaurant if he would partner with me."

"I agreed and threw in what I had. We pitched the idea to a local bank and opened a small place up the road. Two years later we outgrew that and opened another bigger place on Route 1. That did well but needed work so we decided to invest what we had earned in a place closer to the beach and the product is the Stan & Ollie's you see here," Stan finished their story and gestured at the restaurant proudly.

They stood there arm in arm...best buddies...in business together and happy as clams. They were better together than they had been apart and were all the happier for it.

"Good for you. It's good to have dreams and better to see them come true," Reggie said.

"Got to get back to work," Stan said, "Good to see you Joe and glad to have you as a customer and now as a friend, Reggie." Stan & Ollie both shook his hand and headed back to the kitchen.

"Quite a story, huh?" said Joe sipping his coffee.

"Quite a story." Reggie agreed.

They finished their meals and had another cup of coffee lingering and happily wasting some of the day.

"So I'll see you tomorrow morning."

"Sure thing," said Reggie and they headed out.

Reggie had finished his book so he went to the library to turn that one in and get another. There was the latest Clive Cussler book on the new book rack. "Great" he thought. I'll really burn through this one." He took the book to the check out desk and turned over his library card. After the book was checked out, he made his way toward the door.

As he was leaving the library he saw the Goth guy and Peter L'Engle together in the cubicle studying. They both looked up and waved. Reggie waved back and smiled. I guess you can't always judge a book...," he thought staring at the Cussler book he had just checked out. He was hoping that this one was true to what he saw and expected from Cussler's other writing.

"Good book," an older gentleman said. The man was seated on a bench in the morning sun near the library entrance. He had silver hair and a neatly trimmed beard. He was slim and wore a flowered shirt, shorts and sandals.

"Have you read it?" Reggie asked the distinguished looking gentleman who somehow looked familiar.

"You'll really enjoy it. My name's Clive by the way. Have a nice day." The gentleman shook Reggie's hand and walked down the path toward the parking lot.

Reggie looked at the back cover as the man got into a gleaming red, antique convertible and drove off. A smile crossed his face. There on the back of the book was a picture of Clive Cussler...the same man he had just shaken hands with...he had just met Clive Cussler!

Reggie took up a perch on his deck for the rest of the morning. After lunch, he took his beach chair and carrying his umbrella headed to the beach...still reading. Reggie spent the evening on his deck feeling the salty, cool ocean breeze and reading a favorite author whom he had met today. Sometimes life just surprises you.

Chapter 13: Ob-la-de Ob-la-da

Kate Leeman had a busy day planned and as she got ready for work, she ran over that plan in her head. She had some errands to run and two appointments to show houses to perspective buyers. Between appointments and at the end of the day she would do the errands. Between office time, the appointments, and the errands she would be on-the-go all day.

For a few years, the real estate business had been slow in Bethany. She would never tell her boss, but that suited her just fine. She liked a little money coming in that she could spend as she pleased, but she liked the time-off as well so she could work out and bask at the beach. She didn't want to work too hard but she enjoyed the things and the places it bought. Lately though, business had picked up. She was showing more houses, negotiating more rentals on the phone, and generally working all day.

She had not spent much time on the beach this season and it was becoming increasingly harder to set aside time to work out. She liked to work on her body. She wore her make-up carefully and accented her high cheekbones. She kept her body toned and tanned to just the right shade. She was proud of her appearance. She checked herself in the full –length mirror on the back of the bedroom door. She liked what she saw and reached for the dress on the hanger.

Her husband, Frank, enjoyed her looks in private, but was not always pleased when other men looked her way. Frank let it be known that some of the bathing suits and tops she wore did not meet with his approval. 'Well, let him be a little jealous,' she thought, 'it was good for him.' As for the other men or other women for that matter, well she didn't discourage them looking. In fact she enjoyed it. The admiring glances pleased her very much. She finished dressing, checked herself in the mirror once more, and headed out to her car.

Reggie was ready when Joe picked him up. They went to Stan & Ollie's for a quick breakfast and then took up a post down the street from the Leemans' residence. Frank Leeman got into his car a few minutes after they arrived, backed out of the driveway, and left. A half-hour later, Kate Leeman came out of the house did the same. They followed her at a comfortable distance.

Mrs. Leeman drove to her work at Star Realty with Joe and Reggie behind her at a safe distance. She was there for about an hour. The duo then followed her to a house in one of the cottage communities. She met some perspective buyers, showed them the house, and went back into the office. On the way back to the office she stopped at the dry cleaners. Later, she left the office again and met another couple at another house. Mrs. Leeman then went back to the office and stayed there for the remainder of the day. She made another stop at the market before going home at about 3:00PM. Mr. Leeman was already there.

"A blockbuster day, Batman."

"Maybe tomorrow, Robin. I'll pick you up for the funeral...say about 8:30?"

"See you then," agreed Reggie.

The funeral was a town happening. All of the permanent residents were there. The church was filled to overflowing. There was a long procession to the cemetery where Marty McCabe was laid to rest. There were many somber faces as a few discreet photos were taken by the local paper for inclusion in the Bethany News.

---***---

After the funeral, they picked up Reggie's car. Joe took his camera along with the listening device and moved it to Reggie's trunk. When they got to the Leeman house, no one was home.

"How long do we do this for?" asked Reggie.

"In other cases, the spouse tells me when they suspect their husband or wife is cheating on them and I watch on those days and at those times. It's amazing how transparent men or women are when they're cheating on their spouses. They always think they're being so careful. But in this case, Mr. Leeman doesn't know what, if anything, Mrs. Leeman is up to so...I have no idea how long it will take or when to watch. "

"Did you do a lot of this waiting around as a detective?"

"Yes, and it wasn't the best part of the job." Joe went on to tell Reggie a few stories of stakeouts when he was on the police force. This got them talking about other things they had done in their jobs. They got to know each other better as they waited for something...and they didn't know what...to happen.

They only had to wait until early afternoon. Kate Leeman came home and Joe snapped some pictures. A few minutes later, another car pulled into the driveway. A neatly dressed woman got out. The woman was professionally dressed in low heels and a gray dress with black lace trim. She carried a matching handbag, walked briskly to the front door, and rang the bell. The women greeted each other and the second woman went in.

"What have we here," Joe said snapping pictures of the woman.

"Could be just lunch," Reggie said.

"Or maybe she plays for both teams." said Joe.

"You've got a suspicious and dirty mind."

"It's the work I do that has corrupted me. I wish I had put the microphone on the window. I can't because there are no houses nearby and it would be obvious if I walked into the yard, now."

Joe took more pictures about an hour later when the two women came out. The women spoke briefly in the driveway and then got into their cars and drove off. Joe then got out of Reggie's car went around the side of the Leeman house and attached the microphone.

"There, now maybe we can find out what's going on," Joe said getting back in the car. "Let's call it a day."

"How do you know which window to put the microphone on? Do you just guess?" asked Reggie.

"No, Robin. You can see the layout of every house in town on-line."

"No shit, Batman."

Reggie dropped Joe off at his place and enjoyed the rest of the day reading the Clive Cussler book and surveying the ocean from his deck.

Joe and Reggie watched the Leeman house and followed Kate Leeman for several days and at different times. The only thing they learned is that Mrs. Leeman works a lot and that sometimes she comes home in the afternoon and meets with different women. They can only identify one of the women. Rachael Short stopped by once and they both recognized her. It seemed she did nothing out of the ordinary in fact it was very ordinary.

"So what now?" Reggie asked as they were finishing breakfast. "We've seen nothing to even raise suspicion of anything out of the ordinary.

"I'm a bit stumped," admitted Joe. "She doesn't seem to be doing anything that Mr. Leeman would find objectionable. She surely works a lot and she meets with girlfriends. Probably no different than if we were watching Mr. Leeman kibitzing with the town council members and going to his work. I guess it's time to go and talk to him. Maybe he can give us some more information that would help us focus where we might look."

"Good morning, boys. Staying out of trouble?" Chief Stanton said sliding into the booth. "What have we here? Playing voyeur Joe? Taking pictures of pretty ladies? If you post them on the internet you can go to jail for that." He picked up one of the pictures.

"We know who one of them is," Joe said picking up Rachael Short's picture. "But do you know who the others are?"

"This one's Kate Leeman," the Chief said picking up another, "This one's Sue Riddick, and this one's Candy Salter."

"Thanks. Chief," said Reggie. "All we know is that they are all friends of Kate Leeman."

Joe wrote their names on each picture as Chief Stanton handed them back.

"What are you doing taking pictures of town council member's wives? You're going to get into something you might regret. What's going on?"

Joe and Reggie looked at each other with a look of disbelief. What was going on?

Chapter 14: I Get Around

"How were your eggs this morning?" Lexie asked. She did not seem to be her usual chipper self.

"Great as usual," answered Reggie. "Why do you ask?" The Chief and Joe nodded their agreement.

Lexie sat down in the fourth chair with Joe, Reggie, and the Chief. Their regular booth was filled this morning. They had been a few minutes late. "What are you looking at?"

The pictures of the town council wives were spread in front of them on the table and there was discussion as to why the women meet and if there were any patterns to the meetings. Lexie began picking up and studying the photos. She had worry lines on her brow and her smiles this morning had been quick and seemed a bit forced.

"These women are very influential in this town," offered Lexie. "They are all in real estate with various agencies and they are all married to town council members, but enough about them. I need some help," Lexie stated as she put the photos down on the table like a hand of poker. "Well, it's not exactly for me. It's for this new guy I've been seeing."

"Lexie, I'm crushed. I thought I was your one and only," kidded Joe as he feigned a knife through his heart.

Lexie covered Joe's hand with hers. "I know it's hard for you, Joe, but we have to see other people. Seriously, this guy is up against a wall." Her somber demeanor got Joe's attention.

"All kidding aside. What is it, Lexie?" Joe asked.

"His name is Butch Cosgrove. We've gone out a few times and he's a good guy. He was telling me that his business is in trouble. Butch is a local contractor and finish carpenter. He puts in bids for work in town but all he gets are small jobs. He can't seem to nail down any of the big jobs where the real money is. He thinks he's being black-balled or something."

"I know Butch," added the Chief. "He does great work. I've seen some of it. He worked on my kitchen remodel and his work is excellent. He's a fine carpenter himself. He and his crew finished the job on time and on budget. That's a rare combination around here."

"Yes, he gets those types of jobs and he enjoys the work but he can't seem to get big contractor jobs. He says that every time he bids he seems to get underbid by a few dollars and loses out, especially the public work for the town. And then those contractors that do win the bid, run up the price anyway, and the town ends up paying more than Butch bid in the first place."

"So Butch thinks someone is getting inside information so they can underbid him or someone else is just favored?" asked Joe.

"That's what he thinks. Can you help? It's just that he seems a little desperate. The work he gets keeps him in business and some of his crew working but he fears that he will lose some of his best people because he can't supply them with enough work. If he loses them, his business will suffer even more and it's a downward spiral from there."

"Nothing I can do about looking at records being a public servant myself," answered the Chief raising his hands as if to defend himself.

"Sure, Lexie. I'll see what I can find out," promised Joe. "It may take some time but we'll talk to Butch and do some poking around to see what comes up, but these things are usually subtle and hard to prove."

"That's pretty much true. I can't be directly involved but if you need any side info let me know. I've got to go. See you all later," said the Chief as he put on his cap with the scrambled eggs on the brim and headed for the door.

"Thanks, Joe. I'll owe you one." And Lexie gave Joe one of Butch Cosgrove's business cards. "It just doesn't seem fair the way Butch is being treated. There's plenty of work in this town. He just needs to get his fair share. If someone is greedy enough to use these tactics against him...well, I don't think that should happen to a good guy."

"Your undying love is all I need, Lexie. I'll let you know if I find out anything," said Joe.

Lexie left the table and Joe and Reggie looked at each other in silent thought. They pushed around the pictures on the table and worked on silent theories in their heads.

"What do you think these ladies are after?"

"I don't know," Reggie said, "But what I do know is that when you mix politics and business the result is usually something stinky going on. Story after story in Rhode Island follows the same course. The FBI has had a field day of putting crooked politicians in jail over inside deals. They all thought that they were so powerful and considered themselves above the law. Of course they all pleaded that they were working for the public good and trying to make things better for everyone, all the while lining their own pockets with kickbacks. It's almost a way of life…why should this town be any different?"

"I'm not saying it is or it isn't but this all seems pretty peculiar. But I don't see anything tying it all together and maybe its just girlfriends having lunch or female companionship or whatever."

"It could be nothing, but if it quacks like a duck…?"

"Hard evidence, my friend, hard evidence. Anyway," Joe said, "We promised Lexie we'd talk to Butch Cosgrove, so how about we go and do that this morning for a change of pace seeing as how we're getting nowhere with this Leeman thing?"

Using Joe's car, they went to a small shop located in the rear of a cinder block building. This was the home of 'Cosgrove Contractors' indicated by a blue and white sign above the door. Next door, painted on the cinder block wall was 'We fix your shorts'.

"Hey, isn't that Rachael's husband's place?"

"Yeah, quite a logo, huh, pretty juvenile," remarked Joe as they entered Cosgrove's place.

"Good morning," Joe called out. "Hello."

"Hello," came a reply as a man walked in from the back room. "Hi, I'm Butch Cosgrove. What can I do for you?"

"Hi. I'm Joe Finley and this is Reggie Slater." The men shook hands. "We're friends of Lexie's from down at the diner. I'm a retired cop and do some private detective work and we were talking to Lexie this morning and she told us you were having some trouble with contracts. She asked us to talk to you and see if we could help."

"That Lexie. She's a nice girl, but I don't know what you can do."

"We don't either, but why don't you tell us what you think is going on. She seems concerned about you."

"Well, I guess it couldn't hurt. It seems I keep bidding on public projects, you know those given out by the town, and I either get underbid by a few hundred dollars and lose it or I give a real price, get underbid, lose the contract and then there are cost overruns and it ends up costing the town more money in the long run. It would just be bad luck if it happened once or twice but I haven't had any public work, even small jobs, for over two years now."

"Do you think others are getting inside information?"

"That's not supposed to happen because the bids are sealed but who knows? More than that, even private jobs...I seem to get small stuff or partial jobs...enough to keep me in business but I don't get the general contractor jobs where I can make some real money. I don't know if I should move on but going to another state, like down the road to Ocean City, and I would have to get licensed in the state of Maryland. I just don't know what to do."

"Sounds tough; I hear you do nice work," chimed in Reggie.

"That's just the thing. I think my work is top-notch but it doesn't seem to matter. I have all great references and not one complaint from the jobs I've done but I just can't seem to break the ice. I used to get bigger jobs until two years ago and then…about the time this new council was elected…it just dried up."

"So, you think the council is against you?"

"Well, I don't have any proof, but I was supposed to get that Seaside Condo job over two years ago, but Marty McCabe, the town council president that was killed last week, was dead against building it at all. Pardon my choice of words. If it wasn't the environmental stuff it was his restaurant in the way. The council was split on it but he was the deciding vote last time. Now, he's gone and I hear they want to appoint Alan Short to the council, that might at least sway the balance and I might have a chance. Alan's shop is just next door and we get along OK. Maybe he's my way back in."

"I'm not sure we can find out anything but we'll ask around. Small town politics can be a tricky thing. Reggie and I will look into some things and get back to you," Joe said as his back stiffened. "I can't make any promises."

"I appreciate whatever you can do. I can't survive in Bethany Beach much longer like this."

The men shook hands and Joe and Reggie went out to the car.

"Where do you think this is going?" Reggie asked.

"No where good."

Chapter 15: Brown Sugar

"What, another one."

"Easy, Joe. It's just a quick one-day trip."

"If we keep this up, all of the couples in Bethany will be divorced and there will be no more business for you and you'll have to go into real estate," Joe said. "I like the work, Craig, but what don't you understand about *part-time*?"

"You just go up to Philadelphia for a day or two, catch this guy in the act, and come back. It's like a mini-vacation."

Joe, Reggie, and Craig L'Engle were in the lawyer's office late in the afternoon. All of the office help was gone. Craig was telling them about the reconciliation between the guy in the bushes with the broken arm and his wife. She claimed she had never done that kind of thing before and there was a tearful scene right here in his office. They had left arm in arm. That is her arm in his one good arm.

Craig asked, "Would either of you like a drink?" They both nodded and Craig poured all three of them a small scotch, neat. They drank in silence for a few minutes. Then they got back to talking about the new case in Philadelphia.

"So, she's suspicious because he never misses a weekend down here. He's always loved it and now he's missed two in a row. During the winter she started wondering because he worked late a lot but now she's a bit frantic...Actually she's mostly pissed off and wants him to stop and go back to the way it was."

"So you're saying we're in the Good Samaritan business now? Are you thinking of trading in your gavel for a collar?" asked Joe.

"Well, let's just say we're helping her get her life on track."

"You'll have to pay me for the time gone from Bethany and all expenses...for both of us."

"OK...OK. She's willing to pay. She just wants to know. She's stopped here a few times in the last couple of weeks but we've been busy with other cases," Craig explained. "Now he's stayed in Philadelphia two weeks in a row and she's desperate."

"If I'd wanted to be this busy, I'd have hung out a shingle. After this, no cases for at least a week. We need some time to be retired."

"OK. Just get some pictures of them together looking all lovey-dovey. That should do it."

"And one more thing; I need a favor," said Joe.

"You drive a hard bargain. What?" asked Craig.

"We've been nosing around about some contractors' business in town. I know you do some real estate work. Could you look at new construction contracted by the town in the last year and see if there are any patterns?"

"Patterns, like what?"

"Like...I don't know...just if there seems to be anything not quite right with the bidding process." Joe told Craig about Butch Cosgrove and his suspicions.

Craig said, "OK, I'll look and see. I have some title searches to do at the Town Clerk's office anyway. The real estate business seems to be booming here in Bethany."

So it was off to Philadelphia the next morning and now they were sitting outside the guy's house waiting for him to go to work. He went to his office as they expected and Joe and Reggie waited in the car outside hoping this would just be a one-day jaunt.

"What do you think of Lexie's boyfriend?" asked Joe.

"Seems like a nice enough guy...Lexie seems to like him, but she is concerned about his business and if he'll stick around," offered Reggie.

"I can see he's in a tight spot. If he doesn't get work soon, he will be forced to move on. Do you think he's really getting black-balled?"

"I don't know if he's so much getting black-balled or if they just favor other contractors. I guess it just depends how you look at it. That's what makes these things difficult. It's just a matter of choice."

Joe sat quietly and then said," So the council only gives work to their friends...not all that surprising but difficult to prove. The counsel wives seem like a pretty tight group and most of them are in real estate."

"And the biggest real estate project up for grabs right now is the Seaside Condos."

"Yes, but the council has voted that down twice. Doesn't seem to be any undue influence there," commented Joe.

"But it's up for a vote again and there will be a new town Council President and a new Council member. That could sway things."

"And the new member might be Alan Short, Rachael's husband. I'll bet he favors the Seaside Condo project and Butch thinks so, too. Those changes could be the difference for Butch and we're looking into that for nothing."

"And Marty McCabe is dead," Reggie said as the suspect came out of work and got into his car.

"Here we go," said Joe as he followed at a distance. "I hope this guy is horny and we can get back to Bethany tonight."

The guy had brass. They had to give him that. His wife and family were out of town so he didn't figure he had to go to any great lengths to hide anything. He drove right into a neighborhood and pulled into a driveway. A woman greeted him at the door and laid a heavy kiss on him right there. Joe snapped pictures.

The front door of the house closed and Joe got out of the car and went around the back of the house.

"Another microphone?" asked Reggie when he returned.

"Another microphone; the base unit is expensive, but the mics are cheap. I got some great pictures through the back window as well. From the looks of things, we better turn this thing on or the event will be over before we tape anything."

The machine recorded some hot and heavy action. Together with the pictures, it was all the wife would need to confront him.

They packed it up after a half hour and headed back to Bethany. On the way back they called Craig and made an appointment to meet him at the Stan & Ollie's in the morning. It turned out to be a one-day job after all.

---***---

"Mornin', boys. What do you have for me?" Craig asked as he slid into the booth next to Joe.

Joe showed Craig the pictures on his camera's screen that he had taken. "I'll put these on another memory card and get them over to your office. We also have an audio tape of them in the act. I think it will be all you need to satisfy the wife. I don't think his next trip down to Bethany will be all that pleasant."

"No. And if you met her...you'd be scared, too," Craig added.

"Thank you both for going up there. I'll leave you both alone for awhile and let you enjoy Bethany and your supposed retirement. I wasn't totally idle while you were gone either. I had to do those title searches yesterday at the town clerk's office so I looked into public projects over the last year."

"That was quick work. Thanks. Did you find anything that looks shady?" Joe asked.

"Well. You're dealing with two powerful organizations in a small town here. The realtors who are the money that moves the town and the town council that gives out permits that allows new construction. The council approves all bids for public construction and all permits for private building. You see. One drives the other. It's all about the money."

"If there is anything I learned as a cop, it was to always follow the money," Joe said.

"The money seems to go primarily to three big construction outfits in town. They seem to get their private permits approved and get most of the public work over the last two years. The public work is spread among the three pretty evenly but most of the others seem shut-out except for some small, menial contracts that the big firms don't want anyway."

"It always seems to me that everyone is satisfied and everything is great until someone gets greedy," Reggie added.

"Well, let's look at the players. On the town council you have a cast of characters each with their own motivations. There's Chris Donnelly who is now the council president. He owns several beach outfitter and clothing stores. He wants as many people as possible in Bethany because it's good for his business.

"So, he would be in favor of more building no matter what it was," offered Reggie.

"That's right," confirmed Craig.

Frank Leeman is an ultra-conservationist. He supports the cause and works with the local environmental commission. Peter Riddick owns and operates several condominium developments and looks upon new developments as competition and bad for business.

"Those two would be against development," said Joe.

Nate Salter owns the local lumber yard and home improvement store. He likes new developments because they're good for his business.

"So, he loves any kind of building. That sounds like a lot of conflicting interests. I guess that's why this fight over the Seaside condos has gone on for so long," Joe said.

"Funny you should bring that up" Craig injected.

"With Marty McCabe's death, it changes things."

"How so?" asks Reggie.

"Marty owned Sam's restaurant on the beach."

"I know that place. It's right across from my apartment."

"Oh, you got a place down there...lucky you," Craig continued. "Marty's restaurant property was and still is a necessary parcel for the Seaside Condo development. He didn't want to sell. But with his passing, his wife now controls it. I also understand that Alan Short is going to serve out Marty's term..."

"And Alan is married to Rachael who is in realty who favors the development," concluded Reggie.

"And...Jill, Marty's wife, who now owns the restaurant, wants to be rid of it. Jill is also in real estate as are all of the wives of the council members," said Craig.

"Wait a minute," injected Joe. "You're telling me that the balance on the council has now turned in favor of the Seaside Condos and that all of the council member's wives are realtors who all favor the development."

"Candy Salter is a loan officer and not a realtor but yes, I guess I am," stated Craig.

"So, now we've found the money," Joe concluded.

Craig reached for the check but Joe beat him to it. "I'll get this Craig. I think you've earned it. Thanks."

Chapter 16: Do I Have To Come Right Out and Say It?

"What do you think of all that?" Reggie asks. They were still sitting at Stan & Ollie's. They didn't usually stay this long because they occupied a table that Lexie could turn but they were a bit stunned by what Craig had told them before he left for court and needed to talk it out.

"It sounds like a bad soap opera."

"Don't you boys have any crime to fight this morning or do you want more coffee?" it was Lexie nudging them along.

"We'll have more coffee and we'll leave a big tip." Lexie poured. "Lexie, you know a lot of people in this town. What do you know about the town council members' wives?" asked Joe.

"The Bethany Blues?"

"What?"

"The Bethany Blues. That's what they call themselves."

"They have a title?" injected Reggie.

"They have all been coming to Bethany Beach since they were youngsters. Their families owned property here. That's how they got to know each other. They were a bunch of girls that hung around on the beach and started calling themselves the Bethany Blues. There are a lot of groups like that. Once in a while you see a group of middle-aged girls having a reunion...some of them even have t-shirts."

"And all of the Bethany Blues ended up back here?" Reggie thought out loud.

"Yep and they do OK. They got their husbands on the town council and they're all involved in real estate. They make a ton of money and control most of what goes on. They push the property values and push property turnover. They make a commission on every transaction."

"What do you mean they control. They don't hold office."

"They might as well. They lead those wimps around by the short-hairs and pretty much get what they want in the end. Gotta go," and Lexie was off trolling for tips at the other tables.

"I'm making more and more of this all the time," Joe said.

"Can't make this up. Could the girls be that cunning?"

"Maybe we could have listened in on a real town council meeting at the Leeman house the other day and didn't know it," said Joe.

"And maybe Frank Leeman isn't the bundle of nerves we take him for and he's on to something suspecting his wife being involved in some shady dealings. Marty dying like that was a real game changer." Reggie stated.

"Frank doesn't seem like the weak council member Lexie was describing. He maybe a nervous Nellie but he has stuck to his guns voting against the Seaside Condos."

They sat for a time sipping coffee and thinking about all of the things that had happened and then Joe said, "And maybe what we saw out on the county road wasn't an accident."

"Good morning, fellas. Mind if we sit down. There seems to be a shortage of chairs this morning." Two men were standing at their table. The taller one was speaking.

"I'm Chris Donnelly and this is Nate Salter. We're on the town council. We know Joe from around town but you are," Chris Donnelly held his hand out to Reggie.

"I'm Reggie Slater from Rhode Island down here for the summer." Reggie shook hands with both Chris Donnelly and Nate Salter. Their handshakes were typical of politicians...seemingly firm but with no substance.

Lexie came by and the two men ordered. She poured them all coffee and went on her way.

"See you two in here most every morning. Seems you have become friends," Nate said.

"I guess you could say that," Reggie answered.

"This guy," Chris indicated Joe; "Has a bit of a salty reputation around here. He works with that snake Craig L'Engle and gets a lot of guys in...shall we say...sticky situations. Doesn't exactly contribute to the peace and tranquility of Bethany."

"The truth will often set you free," Joe let that just drift into the air.

"Aah, a righteous soul. Sometimes too much truth can land you in a kettle," lobbed Chris. There was a pause in the conversation as they all sipped their coffee.

"There's been talk around that you guys have been asking questions about things that are not necessarily your business."

"And how's that?" questioned Joe.

"Reggie, your new around here so I guess you get a pass, but be warned, Joe, some things just are better left alone. Now you know that the fire is hot, but if you stick your fingers in it, just like your Mama told you, they're going to get burned."

"Yea, my Mama did tell me something like that but, I was never a good listener."

"Let me reinforce that lesson. You've been told." With that Chris threw a twenty on the table and both men got up and left. Lexie was just arriving at the table with their order. She, along with Reggie and Joe, were left a bit speechless.

---***---

"What the hell was that?" Nate asked once they're in the car with the doors closed.

"You know damn well what that was. They're getting too close and had to be warned off. They are outsiders and have no stake in our affairs."

"You think that's going to help?"

"Look, Nate. You're moving up in status on the council and probably the next vice-president. You're now my #1 man. As such, you need to be involved in a little enforcement. Consider this your first lesson. We need to meet with the others and get everyone in line, including the wives so we can contain this thing."

---***---

"What just happened," asked Lexie, standing there with the two plates, "What am I supposed to do with these?"

"I think we just got called to the principal's office," said Reggie who was sweating a little despite the air conditioning.

"Small town stuff, Reggie. Don't worry about it. Let's enjoy brunch on the town."

Lexie put the two plates down and scooped up the twenty.

"Are you guys OK?" Lexie asked looking at Reggie.

"We'll be fine," answered Joe digging into a fresh breakfast plate but Reggie couldn't even look at his dish.

Chapter 17: She's Tired of Boys

"Hi, Deb. How was your day?" Chris asked walking through the door. He needed to keep this pleasant for what was to come. He knew Deb wouldn't like it, but he had to convince her that it was for the best.

Chris Donnelly had spent the day touching base with other council members. They had weighed the stakes and agreed. They needed to circle the wagons and let all of this business calm down. It would go away and in the euphoria of all the profit-making in the summer months, people would forget all about the rumors. In the fall, things would return to normal. They had plenty of time. The election wasn't until November and they had control of the vote until then.

"Deb," he called out again. "Where are you?"

"I'm in here." He followed her voice into the den. She was sitting at the desk. Their den served as sort of a home office for both of them. He took a seat on the sofa. She had changed out of her work clothes and into a t-shirt and shorts. She still had a toned body and looked good in the slightly tight t-shirt. He could tell she was not wearing a bra as her nipples stretched the fabric of the shirt.

"What did you do today?"

"Oh, you know. Ran a few errands...I got a nice steak for dinner tonight...work wasn't too tough. How about you?" she asked. It appeared she was in a congenial mood so he might as well get right to it.

"I talked with the council members today...don't worry...I met with them one at a time so we didn't break any laws. We all agree. There's a problem and we need to address it now."

"What?"

"You know we have the votes for the Seaside Condo development."

"Yes."

"We'll that's what we all wanted but now we have an obstacle." He could see Deb's lips tighten and her neck muscles flex. He hoped this would be the worst. Tread lightly...

"Obstacle! We've been waiting for this for three years. We can only sell the same units over and over so many times. Well, we can sell them a lot but they lose value if there is nothing new to bolster their prices. We need some fresh condos to market and drive the price up to increase our commissions," her voice was getting a little edgy. Chris thought she looked even better when she was a little feisty, but he knew it turned ugly when she reached a certain point. He was feeling that she was not far from that point now.

"I know. I know. Don't get defensive. But that Joe Finley has been poking around and I think he's putting two and two together. I heard that Craig L'Engle was looking at past public permits down at the town hall. This is all getting a little bit hot. I think if we just wait a little longer it will all blow over and we can proceed before November. If we keep pushing and they start talking, everything may..."

"That's too late for next season," her voice was over the edge now. "If we don't get approval until November, we can't even break ground before the spring and that kills the pre-sell during the high season. That delays things even longer." She had reached a crescendo and was about to boil over. He played the last card.

"But it's not just Joe. Craig L'Engle is involved as I said and Joe has a friend Reggie Slater that seems to know all about it, too. It's too wide-spread. We have to contain it."

"You're one vote." He could see steam as she turned in her chair to face him directly. She was breathing harder now and her teeth were clenched. "You've always been in favor. No one will question it." She spoke slowly and deliberately. She continued, "The others will vote as they always have and with Alan...well; now we get the approval. Grow a pair. Get this done and then it will blow over. Who gives a shit about the election? The voters will send you back anyway. Just give the favors like you always do. Make sure they all have a great summer and all this will mean nothing."

There was no debating anymore. She had issued her edict and would not be consoled. Maybe another tack at another time but this wasn't working at all.

"Alright, we'll see how it goes," he said just to appease her for now.

"Damn straight," she said as she got up from the chair and left the room leaving him shaking his head.

He went to the basement Rec room to call the other council members who were slated to vote yes. Things hadn't gone any better talking to their wives and it appeared all of their balls were now in a sling and from more than one direction. He could not reach Alan Short.

---***---

"So they all want to take it off the docket and wait another year?" asked Debbie Donnelly. Her voice was slightly raised and there was a bit of distain in it.

"This is bullshit," said Kate Leeman. They had been talking about their discussions with their husbands about delaying the Seaside Condo project.

Sue Riddick tried to be the voice of reason, "They just want to take it off the docket for this month or two. Maybe this isn't so bad. We'll make out eventually. What difference does it make?"

"I'm not willing to wait. We've made all these plans, set it up...and now we wait...again?" questioned Kate.

"Rachael was a bit more forward, "I'm not willing to delay any longer. I say we put the pressure on now. We made this happen. We've stuck our necks out and if we wait it was all for nothing. No more waiting for the next council or waiting for the fall. I say we make it happen now. Give them no choice."

"I'm with Rachael," said Kate.

"We have been friends for over 25 years. We made plans and here we are at the edge of our biggest success...I say we grab it...squeeze them a little tighter...and make it happen."

There was a lot of murmuring between the girls. The naysayers capitulated and they agreed to put the heat on the men and not to take no for an answer. "We all know what they want. Right, girls. Go home and get on your knees. Resistance will be futile." They all knew that some of the members would never vote yes but, it didn't matter. All they needed was a majority. That's what they always went for. The men never understood or recognized that they were being manipulated because they often times got to vote their conscience. They didn't realize that it didn't matter. The Bethany Blues always got their way.

They all came to the middle of the room and pulled their shirts to expose the top of their left breast. There, on every one of the girls, was tattooed a blue sun. These had been procured many years ago on a night they made the pledge. That pledge brought them all back to Bethany. That pledge bonded them together from their youth to cover for each other and ensure each other's success.

On that fateful night they all gave up their virginity. They had decided they would do it together. Boys had been chosen and manipulated to be together at the appointed time. They had done it together on the beach and later they got the tattoos. It is what made them the Bethany Blues.

Later they left one by one and Kate was left with Debbie.

"I think that went very well," said Debbie tracing the sun on Kate's left breast. Her touch was soft and familiar. Kate leaned in just a little and sighed softly.

"And sometimes, I just can't wait to be alone," moaned Kate as she lifted Debbie's shirt over her head. They embraced and were transported back to a time where they were young and the most intense feelings had been reserved for those closest to them.

"Yes, and sometimes I'm just tired of boys."

Chapter 18: Goin' Out of My Head

Rachael went home thinking in her mind how she would talk to Alan. Sometimes Alan could be so sweet but he was never going to score high on the Mensa test. Sometimes she wondered about him and how she ever...well that was a long time ago. They did alright money-wise because of her job and to be fair his job contributed some. Well, it added to her salary to keep them in touch with the social group she wanted to...no, had to be in. But now they were in a position to really cash in. This had to go right. This had to happen.

Alan cleaned up pretty good and he still could make her shiver sometimes. The way he...well sometimes it was like it used to be.

"Rachael, I'm home." It was Alan, home for the day. OK. She had to look for just the right opportunity to seal the deal with him so he would see it her way. Rachael thought she could bend his will using his weakest point.

"I'm in here, sweetie," she called out.

"I'm going in the shower," he said without even poking his head in. And there it was, opportunity. A girl always had to use her best assets when negotiating. She waited a couple minutes until she heard the shower running and then headed into the bathroom. She removed her clothes and quietly slipped into the shower with him. Reaching around him she began to massage him slowly. He leaned back and moaned a bit.

"You know I missed that." He said. She continued her motion and settled into a rhythm.

After a time Alan turned around and she got on her knees as she had instructed the other girls to do. He was both hard and pliable at the same time. The talk would go easier now.

"Did you talk to Chris Donnelly today?" she asked casually as they were toweling off.

"Yes, he called me at the shop."

"Is everything OK? Why did he call you there?"

"Chris is concerned about the vote next week on the Seaside Condos. It seems some people are poking around looking at permits and bids. He thought that maybe we should wait a bit before we bring the matter to a vote. He wanted to push it off the docket for this month and maybe next month, too."

"And what do you think?" Maybe she had already changed his mind. Better not to play all your cards at once.

"I'm not sure. We're in pretty deep. If it all comes to light: what the council has done in the past, what they want to do, and what you and I have done...well, the whole thing could blow up. I don't want to go to jail."

"You like what I just did." He had been toweling off her back and he suddenly stopped.

"You know I do." He said as he caressed her shoulders.

"Well, if you want to see more of that listen up." Rachael turned to face him. "We and by we, I mean you; are in this up to your eyeballs. If we miss this opportunity, all we've done, all you've done so far might go for naught. The girls all agree; we want this now. Not next month and certainly not next year."

"But what we did with Marty was all your idea. We were only supposed to get his attention; maybe hurt him a little, I didn't..."

"You didn't what? You did it. We may have talked about it, but I didn't make that truck run off the road, you did."

"Rachael, please. I did it because I love you and..." he was pleading now. She had him right where she wanted him.

"Keep showing me you love me by doing what I need you to do," she was speaking softly now and running her fingers through his chest hairs, "And this will end well for all of us and then we'll be on easy street." She stepped back. "You like this house, you like your business," she was driving him backward toward their bedroom, "You like having sex with me...from when we were teenagers and that night on the beach... with all of us...it's been a good life." She pushed him back onto the bed. "We have to stick together now and see it through." She was crawling on top of him as she spoke and he was getting aroused again. Rachael always did this to him. He couldn't refuse her.

"I see your point."

---***---

As Rachael was enjoying convincing Alan to do what she wanted, Reggie decided to take a walk on the beach. Leaving his apartment, the cool evening air surrounded him. It always brought a feeling of contentment to walk the beach in the evening. The sky was still light but an almost half-moon shined. The water still reflected the light of the sky but would soon fade to a darker hue and reflect nothing but the light of the stars and moon. It would be then that night would hug the earth and the earth would return its warmth to the sky.

The Seaside Condo sign on the beach seemed to glare at him. 'Troublemaker ...this will be so nice for everyone...why are you messing with me?' it seemed to say to him. He was concerned and worried. He knew there was nothing that could happen to him, but he wanted to live peacefully here in Bethany and now he was in the middle of this mess. This wasn't part of the plan.

He continued down the beach and saw Joe waving at him from the boardwalk in front of Mango's restaurant. Joe was eating an ice cream cone and beckoning him to join him on the boardwalk. Reggie didn't want to walk into town right then and waved to Joe to join him on the beach. They exchanged a couple of gestures and Joe used the stairs to walk down from the boardwalk and on to the beach. Reggie stopped walking and waited for Joe as he approached.

"You seem a little distant."

"Damn right I'm distant. I come down here for some peace and quiet and look what's happened. I'm not blaming you but this thing seems a bit out of control," Reggie voiced his concern. The meeting with the two council members had rattled him a bit.

"From my perspective as a cop, this is small potatoes." Joe could see that he would have to calm Reggie down some.

"That's just it. You're not a cop anymore and I never was. They were right, the two town council members were right. This is none of our business."

"Reggie, look. There are people in the world that screw over other people. That's a fact. And when they do, someone has to call them on it. They can't just walk and keep doing it. Someone has to stand up and say, enough."

"Joe, it was fine when we were looking for information and piecing some things together, but what can we do now? We have no authority to do more than we have done? We're not cops. We're not on the council. We're barely residents. Our authority or lack of it has run its course."

"I see what you're getting at and maybe you are right. How about we talk to Lamar and see what he thinks. He's a local and he does have the authority to take it further. Maybe our part in this is up."

"Thanks. That's a good idea and would make me feel better. Next time we see him, let's lay out what we have and see what he thinks. At least he should know about that visit we got from the councilmen."

Reggie and Joe walked silently as they made their way down the beach. There were pockets of teenagers congregated at various points. Some were playing Frisbee and football but most were settling in pairs. Some were sitting and talking. Others were making out on blankets. Some sat up as Joe and Reggie passed, but most ignored them. As they got to the other end of the boardwalk, they made their way up and sat on one of the benches facing the surf.

They sat silently for a time and then Reggie asked, "Why can't you see the ocean?"

"What do you mean?" asked Joe.

"Why is it when you sit on the benches can't you see the ocean? The dunes are so high in front of you that if you're seated you can't see. If you stand you can see fine; seems a waste to have these benches here at all."

"Stand up," Joe said and they both got up.

"Now stand at the other end of the bench," Reggie complied. "Now grab the back of the bench and swing it the other way...toward the beach." As they did that, the top of the bench pivoted on the lower part of the base and swung toward the beach. "See, now you can sit and watch the band playing on the bandstand or watch the people going by."

"Now, grab the seat back again and swing it toward the town." Again they grabbed the seat back and swung it back to where it was. Again it pivoted and swung toward the bandstand. "Now, you can sit and watch the ocean." They both sat down and faced the ocean.

"But that's my point," said Reggie. "You can't watch the ocean. You can't see anything but the dune in front of you. Why are the dunes so high?"

"Have you seen the bronze plaques along the boardwalk?"

"The ones with etchings of the various hotels that used to be there and were destroyed by storms?"

"Those are the ones. The dunes are supposed to keep that from happening again. The Army Corps of Engineers came in a few years ago and reclaimed all of the beaches along the coast. Bethany, Ocean City, Dewey, and Rehoboth; they all got a facelift. The Corps dredged beach sand from off shore and put it back on the beach. They changed the shape of the beach to stop erosion and storm damage. Part of that was building up the dunes and that's why you can't see the surf from the benches or observe teenagers at night from here. Super Storm Sandy last year would have done a lot more damage if the Corps hadn't done all this work"

"I still miss the view."

Chapter 19: A Little Help from My Friends

"Hey, Chief, how's things?" Reggie asked as Chief Stanton took a seat with him and Joe. They were having lunch at Stan & Ollie's on this rainy day. Joe had picked up Reggie at his apartment because of the rain. The beach goers were all shopping as a result of the inclement weather and the shop owners were having a profitable day. The beach gets the tourists into town but the rain gets them into the stores. Such is the thinking of retailers.

"Are you ready for this weekend?" Joe asked the Chief.

"Hey, boys. It has sure has been a busy week. Everyone is in town for the 4th of July celebration. The rain has slowed things a bit and I can finally eat lunch today," the Chief remarked heavily taking a seat.

"The rain is at least supposed to clear for tomorrow's parade," Reggie chimed in.

"So they say. Got to love those weathermen. They can be wrong all those times and nobody calls them on the carpet, but they say clearing and I hope they're right. I got everybody on duty tomorrow and I don't foresee any particular problems."

"Speaking about being called on the carpet," and Joe told the Chief about their visit by the town council elders.

"Well. You know they get a bit over protective at times." The Chief was smiling and seemed to not feel that the boys were in any real danger from the threatening nature of the encounter.

"It seemed a little more than that. They seemed to know about Craig L'Engle looking at the permit records and they were pretty adamant that we back off asking any more questions," Joe explained further.

"You can't blame them too much for protecting their turf."

"Well that's just it," continued Joe, "The wives are all in real estate somehow and the town council controls the permits. It all seems a little bit like incest to me. And if we're following the money in all this, it seems that it all centers right there," said Joe.

"I'll admit that it seems a bit peculiar," Lamar explained, "but this is a small town and the same people wear many hats. There's bound to be a lot of overlap, like you're seeing with this. I think you might be reading a little more into this than is there. We're not a big city like Philadelphia, you know."

"What you're saying may be true, but then you have the weird quirk of fate of Marty McCabe's accident."

"You're not going to start that again."

"No, hear me out. What if it wasn't an accident and it wasn't his fault either?"

"Don't you think that's a bit of a stretch?"

"This can only be about two things...sex or money and maybe we have both here. People are paying way above the mean price for property here in Bethany. It seems like prices are being driven up by some unknown force. That force means nothing but increased profits in commissions for realtors and loan officers."

"Chief, we have our suspicions but we're bringing them to you because there's nothing else we can really do and we could use your help," Reggie explained hoping that the Chief was feeling more sympathetic towards their thinking.

"I don't know what I can do but I'll mull it over. It's bothersome, but I don't think it's anything, but you never know. So between shooing teenagers off the beach and supervising tomorrow's parade, I'll think about it. I can't think about too much until after the parade. As far as profits...people just get into bidding wars over properties. It's silly, I know, but if they want to overspend for property here in Bethany neither you nor I is going to stop them. I guess we're a victim of our own success. People, people like you Reggie, just want to be here."

The group sat quietly for a few minutes, thinking to themselves. It seemed that they all had said all they wanted to for now and further discussion would just lead to disagreement and they didn't have enough evidence for any resolution.

Reggie finally broke the ice by changing the subject. "I thought the point was to get people on to the beach. What's with shooing teenagers off the beach?"

"The beach is the main attraction but not at night and not for the reasons those kids are out there."

"And what's that?" asked Joe.

"It starts off innocent enough but public nudity and having sex on the beach, most of it by under aged kids, is a national past time here in Bethany," the Chief informed them. "We're not voyeurs mind you; we use big lights so they see us coming."

"Why do it at all? It must sap your manpower."

"It does. It does. But it concerns the town council, so we do it. The counsel tries to keep things clean even though most of their children were probably conceived the same way. You boys have a nice day and try to stay out of trouble." The Chief had finished his breakfast. He drained his coffee mug and headed for the door saying his goodbyes as he left.

"What do you think? "asked Reggie, "Did that do any good?"

"I'm not sure...probably not. Maybe we could attack this from a different angle.

"I don't know. What would that be?" Reggie could see the wheels turning inside Joe's head.

"Hear me out. You want to buy a condo, right."

"I don't want to pay rent forever and I probably can't count on the unit I'm renting now for next season. I'd love to buy it, but I don't know if they want to sell or if I can afford it."

"How about we make the realtors force the issue for us?"

"How do we do that?"

"All you have to do is to go shopping. Go shopping for a condo with very specific requirements."

Chapter 20: Playing with Fire

"Good morning Rachael. Good morning Tammy." Reggie had walked up through town to the Blue Sky Realty office and both women were at the counter as he walked in.

Good morning, Reggie," Rachael replied, "Good to see you again."

"Hi, Reggie," added Tammy.

"What can we do for you today? Is the rental OK?" asked Rachael.

"Oh, yes. Everything is great and I'm enjoying it very much. I like to talk to you about buying a place. Sort of an early shopping; look see."

"Come on back to my office and we'll see what we can find. We're only open a couple of hours this morning because of the parade." Reggie followed Rachel back to her office enjoying the smile Tammy gave him as he passed.

Rachael sat behind her desk and Reggie sat in one of the client chairs. "Blue Skies Realty has a float in the parade and I'm in charge this year. After this I have to get to the beach parking lot and make sure things are ready. So, you want to become a resident down here."

"I thought it might be beneficial for tax reasons and to be here more than just the summer season," Reggie said. He had been contemplating this anyway so he didn't have to make up a story.

"You're right. Delaware does have some tax benefits over Rhode Island and many owners declare their residency down here just for that reason...especially retirees. If you buy any piece of property, you can have your retirement pay sent here. Once you do that, you are a resident for tax purposes. Your retirement pay goes up and your taxes go down. It's a win-win."

"Exactly why I'm looking."

"The other reason to have your inquiry on file is at the end of the season several properties come up for sale but they are snatched up quickly. If I know what you want and a property comes on the market, I can put a hold on it for you and give you a call. That way you don't miss out."

"Just what I was thinking." OK. Reggie had her interested as most real estate agents would be...this may not be as hard as he thought. All he had to do now is get his requirements to be specific and lead her to the right conclusion.

"Do you want a place like you are in now?"

"Well, my first thought would be is... can I buy that place from the owner?" Reggie and Joe had thought this would be the most logical thing to ask. It would be unlikely the owner would sell and that would lead to the next step.

"I don't know. Like I told you that ownership is a partnership and it would require the approval of both owners and you would probably have to have some sort of a contract about rentals and usage with the remaining owner."

"I see. That might be complicated, but could you ask?"

"Sure. No harm in that. But it did seem that the owner's wife's health problems were temporary. But, I'll ask. Beyond that, if you looked for another place...are looking for the same layout?"

"No, not exactly. This place is nice and I'd buy it if it is available but I can't have people visit and put them up. One visitor could sleep on the couch but that's it. I would like a place with two bedrooms, one and a half baths, an eat-in kitchen, and a sitting room. A big plus would be a deck with a view of the ocean." Reggie was reciting the description from the sign of the Seaport Condo development. This was the bit suggested by Joe."

"Well, that won't be cheap."

"I know but it will be permanent and I have a good down payment and can pay for it over time. My credit rating is good and I might even sell my place in Rhode Island and move down here full time. I have plenty of equity in the Rhode Island property and I'm not really interested in rental options."

"Again, I'll have to do some research. I really don't have enough time today to do a good job with this," she said as she finished up her notes. "Is it ok if I get back to you in the next few days? This is a whole different database and like I said, it might be best to have this go into the early fall when more properties are on the market."

"I understand," said Reggie. "I can afford to be somewhat patient, but I sure would like to have something secure for next season before I go back to Rhode Island."

"OK, I got it. I'll be contacting you over the next couple of days."

"Fair enough. You have my cell." And with that Reggie bid Terry a good day in the outside office and left Blue Skies Realty. The hook was now baited.

---***---

The day was full of festivities. For the parade, the local businesses and homeowners had constructed floats. This was tradition in Bethany. It was a competition among families to come up with the best float. Men, women, and children helped in the construction and rode on the floats in costumes. Most were Independence Day themed, but some were just outrageous.

There was the usual Uncle Sam and the local VFW band. There were Star Wars characters and Ninja Turtles. But this year's best idea, at least in Reggie's estimation, was a family that had dressed as lobsters. They rode on a float decorated as the bottom of the ocean and sang and danced "Under the Sea" from "The Little Mermaid."

The townspeople and vacationers lined the streets as the parade passed shouting and clapping their encouragement. The local high school band marched and groups of flags and twirling batons accompanied them. It was all a matter of pride in an all-American town.

Later that evening, Reggie strolled down to the bandstand at the end of Garfield Parkway to listen to the music. It was a pleasant night and a grand setting. The end of the parkway was a park unto itself. The bandstand had been constructed as part of a town owned structure with bath houses in the rear. The stage was open toward the beach with a large bricked area with white benches. When sitting you could see the band, up Garfield Parkway with the town on both sides, and the ocean was behind you. It was a magical scene created by the town and pictured on many postcards.

"Is this seat taken?" asked a pleasant looking woman. Reggie was sitting on a bench at the Bethany bandstand listening to the concert. This week's special performance was 60's, 70's, and 80's rock performed by a band called *Remember It Well*. The members of the band were all the same age as their rock music implied. They tried all the moves to go with the groove but at their age Reggie was wondering if the EMT's were on duty for the crowd or the band members if they threw out a hip.

"No, no it's not. Please, sit down," answered Reggie. Looking at her a bit more closely as he feigned listening to the music, she was more than a pleasant looking woman. It was hard to guess her age...she was in good shape, with a fine bronze tan. This was accented by her blond hair, cropped in a short summer style, and a loose, white flowered dress that was about knee length. She had a strong chin and lipstick that was a light pink on full, soft lips matching some of the color in her dress. Her knees were nice, too.

She caught his glance once and smiled. She caught him looking a second time and turned towards him, "Do you like the music?"

"I...I...do," he stammered like a schoolboy. "What do you think of it?"

"I like it fine but I would rather walk on the beach and listen. Want to come with me?"

"Sure, I'd like that," Reggie answered quickly and got up. She remained seated extending her hand. Reggie reached for it to help her up. She did not release his hand immediately and she felt warm to the touch. They walked from the band area and down the walk way that led through the dunes and to the beach. She stopped at the end of the walkway and extended her hand once more to steady herself as she removed her sandals. She held on while he also removed his.

They walked the surf line sending the small sandpipers scurrying as they approached. The surf cooled their feet as they sunk into the wet sand.

"I have not seen you here before," she stated.

"I retired from a Rhode Island school system about three weeks ago. I am renting a beach house here in Bethany. Do you live here or are you just vacationing."

"I live here now. I moved here about five years ago. I'm a manager at a condo complex in Ocean City down the road. One of the condos is a residence for the manager. It's a perk that goes with the job."

"Sounds like a nice set up."

"It is, but it's hard to get away. There has to be someone on call 24/7. My assistant manager is covering tonight."

"There's so much in Ocean City. Why come to Bethany?"

"For the music...no, it's just a diversion. Ocean City is so busy and I see many of my clients while I'm out. The condo building is a huge complex on the beach. Bethany is much quieter and I can be myself here and meet interesting people, like you. My name is Sandra Fleming, nice to meet you..."

"I'm Reggie Slater...the pleasure is all mine." and their hands touched again and lingered. Have you had dinner, Sandra?" Reggie tried out her name. It fit her face.

"No, Reggie," he liked the way his name sounded when she said it. Their hands were still touching. They had stopped walking now were just standing in the surf facing each other.

"Would you like to have dinner with me tonight?"

"I would very much. How about we walk up to the Parker House and see if they have a table tonight?"

Reggie was pleased with her choice of restaurant. If she wanted a more public place, she would have chosen Mango's. But to chose the Parker House meant that she wanted something more intimate and quiet. He couldn't believe his luck. "That's a great choice. I'd love, too."

They retraced their steps and passed across the seating area for the band stand. The band was on a break and people were milling around, going in and out of the stores, and getting ice cream. They talked little on the way and Reggie held the restaurant door for her.

"Good evening, Pauley," Sandra said to the host in the Parker House. "Do you have a quiet table for me and my friend Reggie here," she said touching his arm as she said his name.

"For you, Ms. Fleming, of course. Right this way." Who was this woman? Reggie thought.

They passed by a girl playing her guitar by the bar area seated on a stool. Other diners were conversing in hushed tones. The Parker House was not a loud place and a bit more upscale here in Bethany. The Beatles tune "Yesterday" floated softly over the crowd as they made their way.

"Will this do?" asked Pauley as he pulled out her chair.

"This is wonderful. Thank you, Pauley." Sandra gave him a wide smile as a thank you and she and Reggie sat down. The table was just far enough away from the music to be pleasant but not too loud and just a touch secluded. Reggie slipped Pauley a tip as he shook his hand before he sat. The female guitarist sang softly and her voice was as pleasant as her guitar.

"So, how long are you here for?"

"I rented the condo until at least Labor Day and I can stay longer if I want. I'm also shopping for something more permanent?

"Oh and how is that going?"

"I've only just started looking and I'm waiting for the realtor to get back to me," answered Reggie.

"Well if you're lucky, you'll catch someone selling at the end of the season."

"That's what I thought."

"And you're all set up down in Ocean City?"

"Yes. It's a nice condo but it is contingent on the job. I used to live in Philadelphia and I've always been in hospitality. I have one grown daughter that still lives there. I divorced about 10 years ago and my ex lives in Texas. We're friendly but don't communicate much. And you?"

"I've never been married and thus have no children. I was a principal when I retired but I was ready to be done with it and try something new. I'd like to sell the condo I have in Rhode Island and move here permanently. I have someone living in it now." As he spoke, his leg brushed against hers. She did not move it and now their legs were touching under the table.

"The waitress appeared and they ordered drinks and dinner. "Do you think some things just happen?" Sandra asked.

"What do you mean?"

"Well, you came here for the summer and went to that band concert tonight and sat on that bench. I got bored at home and decided to come up here to Bethany, heard the band, and sat on that bench with you. Isn't that what they call kismet?"

"I guess you could say that and yes, I believe many things just happen. It's just that we don't see them all as an opportunity," Reggie said.

"Is that what this is an opportunity?"

The waiter came with their wine.

Reggie held up his glass as did she. "An opportunity to have dinner with a beautiful, seemingly connected, woman." Their glasses clinked and they drank.

Their dinner came and it was delicious. They talked softly as they ate. Reggie insisted and paid the check and they walked outside.

"I really should be getting back to Ocean City. The evening was lovely. Thank you for dinner."

"It was my pleasure and thank you for making the evening so pleasant."

She linked fingers with him as they walked up the street until she stopped, "This is me," she said pointing at a light blue Camry parked in front of them. She turned and entwined her fingers in his other hand. She leaned in and offered him a soft kiss on the lips which lingered for a moment. "Thanks again, "she breathed and released his hands.

Sandra dug into her shoulder bag and came out with a business card. "This is my work number and on the back is my cell," she said writing her cell number on the back. She offered him the card in one hand and another card with the pen in the other, "And your number?"

Reggie took the pen and the card and wrote his cell number on another card then gave it back.

"I would really like to see you again soon," Reggie said.

"Call me next week. We'll see if we can set something up for the weekend." Sandra got into her car and backed out of the space. They both waved as she drove off. Reggie couldn't believe his good luck. He felt like one of those boys on the beach.

Chapter 21: Hot Legs

On Sunday, Reggie had planned...well, he hadn't planned. He wanted to do very little. That was his plan. He ate breakfast at home because the diner would be packed with the Sunday crowd and most of the guys didn't go on Sundays anyway. He grabbed his book and headed for the deck. On the way out, he found a folder jammed into his screen door. It was from Rachael. Late last night or early this morning she must have left some property sheets for him to look at.

He took the folder and his book and stretched out on the lounge to read, watch the ocean, and feel the breeze. It would be a full day. He looked through the papers Rachael had left. There were some nice and some not so nice places. The prices were of course high but he expected that. There were two or three pictures printed with each property along with the specs. He sorted through them and ended up with five condos that interested him. Of the five, two only had one bath, two were on the far side of town, and one was decent. He would have to call Rachael on Monday.

He settled in with his book, looked at the ocean, and felt the breeze. This was life in Bethany. He had been enjoying the peace for a couple of hours when the phone rang. Thinking it might be Sandra, he answered.

"Hello."

"Good morning Mr. Slater, this is Debbie Donnelly. I heard you are looking for a condo in Bethany."

"And how did you hear that," Reggie inquired.

"We have a very cooperative realtor network here in Bethany and we tend to help each other out. Did you know that not all realtors have access to the same properties?

"No, I didn't know that."

"I thought it might be good if we talked and I showed you some of the properties that we hold exclusively. I think it might be very helpful in your search."

"Well, I'm just lounging on the deck today..."

"That's OK. You don't even have to get up." And there she was at the top of the stairs. She was dressed in white high heels, short black skirt, and a white blouse that didn't leave a whole lot to the imagination. Her jet black hair flowed to her shoulders. Her wide smile and red lipstick added to that come-hither look. It looked like that was exactly what she was going for in the first place. If it was, she had one hell of a sales pitch.

Taking her phone from her ear and hanging up with her thumb she said. "I have some properties right here that I think might fit the bill for you right now. Let me show you. Could we go inside? The sun is rather bright and it would be best if we could lay these pictures out on a table so they won't be blown by the breeze." She was holding a folder in her hand and waving it toward his apartment door.

Reggie got up from the lounge and opened the door for her. She went in and started laying pictures on the table. She didn't seem too concerned that her skirt was riding up revealing her long, tanned legs.

Debbie always kept her "ear to the ground." Finding new clients was not hard but it was fiercely competitive. She had always been used to having and getting what she wanted. Sometimes it caused friction with other real estate agents but she knew how to land a new client.

Landing "new" clients was the name of the game. Once someone became a client and you made that first sale; it led to more. If the client wanted to buy or sell another property; they called you back. You were their agent...their "go to" person. They told their friends about you and got you more clients. Yes, the new client was paramount to being successful even if it rustled a few feathers. Being married to Chris, now president of the town council after Marty was killed in that unfortunate car accident helped a lot by keeping her connected to inside information. Chris also provided an avenue of influence with town politics that drove development and kept the real estate business fresh.

Debbie knew that selling real estate was a game...a very profitable game...especially for agents. They collected commissions if houses were sold...Agents collected fees if properties were rented. Then the properties were bought and sold again. Buying...selling...buying...selling...meanwhile collecting commissions every time. Agents were necessary to the process. The client couldn't do it alone and paid handsomely, every time, for the service.

And Debbie Donnelly was a good and practiced agent that used all of her talents to the best advantage..."We have exclusive access to these properties. They are similar to what you have now," she said looking around, "And we can talk price if you find something you like. The asking price on the sheets is just a place to start the negotiation."

Reggie started looking through the pictures that had descriptions on the bottom just like the ones Rachael had given him. In fact, some of the properties Ms. Donnelly was showing him were ones that he had already seen in Rachael's stack. This must be a cut throat business. Even supposed friends and colleagues would go behind each other's back and lie. It was all about the money, like Joe had said.

He divided them as he had divided the others. He was left with a few that he found interesting and had them side by side.

"Let's both sit on one side of the table so we can look at them," said Ms. Donnelly and she pulled her chair around and sat next to Reggie. She sat rather close and she smelled good too. "Besides," she continued, "Properties that others handle, we can get you a better price."

"And how do you do that, Ms. Donnelly?"

"Please. Call me Debbie, Reggie. We get you a better price because we negotiate with the seller and we can often convince them to lower the price for a quick sale rather than having it on the market for a long time." As she spoke, she leaned in closer and Reggie felt the toe of her shoe rubbing against his leg. Also more of her cleavage became exposed. Debbie made no attempt to hide it...she knew how to use her talents.

"We can also offer great benefits to the buyers." Now it wasn't her shoe but her bare foot that was rubbing his leg and Reggie was beginning to understand the benefits she was talking about.

"I see your point about the benefits and I appreciate what you are offering, but I was dealing with Rachael first. I do feel that I should give her first shot. If she can't find me something I want, then maybe we can do business."

"That's a nice sentiment, but it doesn't get you or me what we both want." She was still working her way higher on Reggie's leg, now with her hand, and leaning in closer. "I know of a place being built for occupancy next year. I can get you a preconstruction price that no one else can match," she cooed. "But you have to act fast to get in on the ground floor so to speak. And if you act now, there are other benefits that can be attached to the deal as well." Debbie breathed the last part into his ear. It was becoming more difficult to concentrate. Reggie tried to hold it together and get more information.

"And where is this place located?" Reggie led her on. Debbie's motions continued and Reggie struggled. He forced himself to focus on drawing the actions of these women to light. Debbie was driving a hard bargain in more ways than one.

"Right on the water here in Bethany," she continued, "Actually not far from here." She sounded like she was getting aroused all by herself. Reggie thought the best way was to get right to the point and end this quickly. He really didn't know if he could hold it together too much longer.

"You mean the Seaside Condos down the street. I've seen the sign."

"Yes, I do sweetie," now she was breathing in his ear again. I can get you an insider's price. Just make me your agent and I'll really work for you."

"I thought that project was stalled." She was rubbing higher on his leg and he was growing weaker by the moment. The closeness of her body was very distracting.

"I happen to know that it is definitely on again and will come up at the next council meeting. It's a lock," she said with surety.

"I might be interested if I see the permits go through, but I'm not so sure that it's a lock for the next council meeting."

"Oh, believe me honey, it's a go," she seemed to be losing her enthusiasm. "But if you aren't interested..."

"I'm interested. It's just that Rachael..."

"I know. You were dealing with her first," she got up and straightened her skirt. The tone of her voice had become angered. "Hey, when she leaves you with nothing come and see Debbie. I'll take care of you, but it will cost you and no special treatment. This was just a one-time offer." And with that she gathered her papers and left.

The trail of her perfume was still in the air. Reggie felt like he had just walked through a pit of asps and couldn't believe he was still alive. But she did smell good.

Chapter 22: Every Picture Tells a Story

"This is the only condo that interests me out of this group." Reggie had called early on Monday and made an appointment with Rachael to discuss the units that she had dropped off. He needed to frame his argument carefully to see what she would offer him once the pressure was on to make the sale.

"What was it about the other choices that eliminated them, Reggie?"

"Rachael, if I'm going to buy, I want exactly what I'm looking for without compromises. I intend to occupy that condo for a long time and I'd like to buy exactly what I want." He tried not to be intimidating, but polite and firm in his desires for the unit he wanted.

"I see. I'll set up a tour of this one that you chose. Oh, I contacted the owner of the unit you're in and his wife is doing much better. He thinks they'll be down next year so he doesn't want to sell. He says though if he doesn't come, he'll rent it to you for the summer."

"That's good to know. If I don't find anything to buy, it could be a good fall back."

"I do have another idea. How about a new unit? The price would be a bit higher but you get exactly what you want in the location I know you want."

"Tell me more."

"I'm sure you've heard about the Seaside Condo development."

"Well, yes, I've seen the sign but I thought that was held up by environmental concerns," said Reggie. This was a well rehearsed response, but he didn't want to pressure her too much and so left the other option open for now.

"That's true but I have it on good authority that those problems will be cleared up soon and the units could be ready for summer occupancy next year."

"Well, that would be great but how can you be so sure?"

"My husband is now on the council and he tells me that it is a go and it's on the docket for the next council meeting. I think it's safe to say that we can start offering some preconstruction sales...pending the approval of course."

"I don't know. It sounds kind of iffy to me."

"Let me show you some of the design drawings for a unit like you are describing." She laid out beautiful color drawings of a condo unit with a great kitchen, sitting room, two bedrooms, and two baths. There was also a view shown from an imaginary deck...just what he had asked for.

"These really are beautiful. What kind of price are we talking?" They talked about price, discounts, preconstruction discounts, down payments, and monthly payments. It was all pending approval of the council of course.

"I can get you the best deal here," Rachael said.

"Funny. That's what Debbie Donnelly said."

"What! When did you see her?"

"Yesterday, she stopped by my place."

"How did she even know you were shopping?"

"She said all of the realtors in Bethany shared customer information. It seemed like she was just trying to help."

"I'd be careful if I were you. Debbie Donnelly can be a little shifty. Besides, you came to me first and I've been working for you. Haven't I?"

"Yes you have. And I told her that I owed you because we have been working together, but she offered me some other incentives."

"If I know Debbie, I'm sure she did."

---***---

"But Craig, could these women be as powerful as all that?" asked Joe.

"From their position in the realty business and their relationship with their husbands who control the political side, why not?" answered Craig.

Reggie, Joe, and Craig were in Craig's office putting some finishing touches on some pending cases. They each had a drink and were throwing around speculation about the Seaside Condos. It was after business hours and the office help had departed for the day.

"Have you never read Lysistrata? Women can make men do anything if they can get them thinking with their little head instead of the big head with the brain they were born with...like the Viagra commercial says...it's a question of blood flow...or lack of it," Craig analyzed.

"What?" asked Joe; now looking confused.

"Lysistrata is an ancient Greek play by Aristophanes in which the women withhold sex from their husbands until they get what they want. Maybe it shows how a true democracy works. And that was a story based in ancient Athens, Greece, known as the birthplace of democracy," explained Reggie.

"That sounds like how many households work from what I understand, but what about the change in balance on the town council?" Joe threw that out for discussion.

"Maybe it was just a stroke of luck for them that Marty met that tree," said Craig.

"I have a feeling that luck had nothing to do with it," Joe said.

"Rachael sure jumped in and nominated her husband Alan to complete Marty's term before the body was even cold," added Reggie.

"It just seems all too convenient," questioned Joe. "The pieces fall in place too easily for it to be happenstance."

"Could they have planned it all along? Manipulated the whole thing," asked Craig.

"What do you mean planned? Like they wanted Marty out of the way and made it happen?" said Reggie.

"Well, the Seaside Condo development is or will be a big money maker for the real estate ladies...otherwise known as the Town council wives...otherwise known as the Bethany Blues. Marty stood in their way. He was the one vote stopping things from moving along. Change Marty's vote and the Seaside Condo development gets a permit and the Sam's restaurant property get acquired...it's like a two-for-one." Craig offered this for the speculation of the group.

"Are you suggesting they would have Marty killed to get what they want? Isn't that a bit much...even for mean girls?" commented Reggie.

"People have been killed for less in my experience. The question is...what should we do now?" offered Joe.

"We need to get the Chief in on this. We need something more to convince him," Reggie said.

"You're right, Reggie. What could we bring to Lamar to get him to work with us?" Joe put in.

""So, it seems there is motive here...where is the opportunity?" offered Craig from the lawyerly side.

"The opportunity lies in the accident with Marty's truck and the tree," said Joe.

"No one could manipulate the tree, so what about the truck?" Craig said.

"The truck...we need to take a look at the truck," stated Joe.

"Where is the truck?" asked Reggie.

"The town has an impound yard out behind the police station. The truck has probably been there since the accident," said Craig.

"We'll have to talk to Lamar just to gain access. Maybe he'll let us into the impound yard just to shut us up," offered Joe.

"That seems like a good angle," said Reggie as he finished his drink.

---***---

"I don't like it. I told you to leave it alone."

"But, Lamar. We just want to look. Whatever we find or don't find we'll bring it to you. No information leaves our lips to the outside world unless you know it and OK it first."

"Joe, you know I trust you; but Marty was a friend and I don't want his reputation sullied for no reason. Whatever you find comes right back here. Nothing leaves this office without my OK. If there's nothing there, will you give this up?

"If I find nothing useful beyond what we already know...then I'll shut up."

"Then OK. Come back tomorrow. It'll be better in the daylight. I'm looking forward to taking you up on your offer to shut up."

Chapter 23: Start Me Up

"We're going to own this town, Deb."

"I can see it now," said Kate. "Twenty or twenty-five years from now, the Bethany Blues girls on the town council, owning restaurants, businesses, and stores we'll have a great future if we stay together."

"I'd like to open a boutique on Garfield Parkway," said Debbie. "Maybe even my own line of beach wear. Women would come to Bethany just to shop at my store." Debbie stood up and pretended to walk the fashion runway. The other girls laughed with her.

"I think I'd like to be in politics. I could be the town council president. Of course the business climate under my administration would be favorable to you all," added Jill. She said this in a serious tone while she banged a fictitious gavel.

"I bet Sue would be a great restaurateur. We could have a permanent table at her restaurant," offered Kate.

"We would be the Chamber of Commerce and meet there once a month. And Candy would be our president and own the local real estate office." added Sue. Candy stood up and took a bow.

"That's where the money is," agreed Candy. "We could all make a killing in real estate."

"That's where I want to be," said Rachael. "I don't want to depend on a man to define my life. I want to be my own person and rule my own domain." She spread her arms as if to embrace the world.

The girls were on the beach. The sun was setting and the darkness was falling all around them. They were sitting closely on a blanket facing each other. It was toward the end of summer and there had been many nights that they spent the evening on the beach talking. They were close; as close as sisters; maybe closer. They had met here, grew up here, matured here, the place defined them. They were now in their late teens and headed off to college next year. Their association together had come to define them to all that knew them.

"Let's make a pact to come back," said Rachael.

"What do you mean?"

"Come back to Bethany. Not just for a reunion when we're 40 years old, but come back here to live and control our own destiny," Rachael looked at all of them and tugged at her shirt to reveal the tattoo of the blue sun above her left breast.

It was the summer of their senior year in high school. They knew their presence in Bethany would be sporadic for some of them over the next few years. To remain true, they all knew they needed something more to hold them together. They were already bound by their past but they need a goal for the future that would act as a magnet to pull them all back.

One by one each of the girls exposed the tattoo of a blue sun at the top of their left beast and with their free hand put their fingers on the tattoo of the girl next to them.

"So, then it is done," said Rachael.

"It's done," they all repeated.

Night fell on the group and the sand gave up the heat of the day to the cool night air and there was a chill that passed over the beach.

---***---

"Where do we start, Joe?"

Reggie and Joe were in the impound yard behind the police station.

"Put these on," Joe said handing Reggie a pair of latex gloves. "We have to be systematic about this. Whatever we are looking for is not obvious because others did not see it. It could be something out of place or something not there that should be so look at everything for what it is and where it is." Joe knew there was a good chance of finding something because other investigators had looked with the mindset of Marty McCabe driving drunk down the road into a corn field. Joe and Reggie were looking with the thinking that someone had helped him into that situation.

"OK. So I'm on the driver's side. You take the passenger side. Here's a penlight to help you see in the darker areas. What do we know so far," Joe asked as he began to search at the dashboard on the driver's side. Reggie made his way around the wreck and yanked on the passenger side door.

"Marty McCabe is dead and Alan Short is on the council."

"And about the accident?"

"The truck ran off the road." started Reggie.

"And it didn't slow down."

"And there was booze involved." Reggie ran his hands over the passenger side dash and shined his penlight under the dash to look there.

"Booze and speed; a deadly combination," said Joe.

"The truck went airborne and hit the tree."

"And booze bottles were broken."

"And so was Marty McCabe."

"Everything in the truck went forward when it hit the tree."

"And some of it went back as it bounced off of things in the truck."

"Including Marty McCabe."

"And including the broken glass from the booze bottles and the booze."

"Which spilled all over Marty McCabe."

"And the top from this bottle of booze," Joe said as he reached under the driver's seat and came out with the broken top to a bottle. "What's wrong with this picture?" He held up the neck of the bottle for Reggie to see. Reggie picked up the largest piece of the matching bottom of the Knob Creek bourbon bottle from the passenger floor.

"A broken bottle. Marty was drinking we know that."

"Do we?" asked Joe. "Look again."

Reggie looked at the bottle of Knob Creek bourbon in his hand. "Good stuff," he said.

"Yeah. Good stuff Knob Creek. But did he drink any of it?" Joe asked.

Reggie looked and then he realized, "No, no he didn't."

---***---

"Chief, I think we've got something," Joe said as they walked into Lamar's office. He wasn't alone. "Aah, sorry Chief.

"Lieutenant, could you give us a few minutes. And could you please close the door on the way out?"

Lamar seemed a bit miffed with them and took a seat behind his desk. When there was just the three of them, Joe, still wearing the latex gloves, laid a towel on the Chief's desk and opened it.

"What's this?" asked the Chief.

"We found this in Marty's truck. The top was under the driver's seat and most of the rest of the bottle was on the passenger's-side floor."

The Chief studied the pieces. "What do you think this means, Joe?"

"I think it means that Marty might not have been drinking at all. Look. The bottle top is still sealed. Knob Creek bottles are sealed with a black plastic substance that you have to peel off in order to unscrew the cap. The seal is still in place."

"I see. So if it wasn't alcohol, what put him into the tree?"

"All we have left is speed or..."

"No, Marty wasn't the type. He was on top of the world and would not have ended his own life."

"So, we're left with speed that caused the accident," Reggie added.

"But Marty wouldn't have kept his foot on the gas right through the corn field right up until he hit the tree. That just doesn't make any sense," said the Chief.

"Right. It doesn't make sense," said Joe. The three of them stared at the broken bottle lying on the towel.

"OK, there are apparently other forces at work here, Joe."

"We were talking with Craig yesterday."

"You got a lawyer involved...that's all we need."

"Easy, Chief. We didn't get a lawyer involved in any official capacity. We were just mulling over what we knew."

"And what do you know?"

"We know Marty's dead and Alan is taking his place on the council."

"Yeah."

"And we also know that the Seaside Condo project will probably get the permits at the next meeting."

"You might be right about that."

"And we followed the money and this is where it led," Joe said as he held up the top of the still sealed whiskey bottle.

"You are right about that."

---***---

"You bitch."

"Whoa! Easy there, Rachael."

"Deb, you violated the code...you stepped over the line..."

"I was just trying to drum up some business. We've been a little slow lately and my boss was on my back to make a couple of quick sales. You know how it is."

"No, I don't know how this is and we never screw each other over. You know better than that. Or maybe you don't."

"Yes...I do. I'm sorry. I was desperate."

Debbie Donnelly had picked up the phone knowing it was Rachael. She knew it was coming, but she was still taken aback by the strength of Rachael's vocal rebuke.

"And did you mention the Seaside condos to Reggie?"

"Yes, I was trying to give him what he wanted."

"I know what that means coming from you. You need to straighten up Deb. You know we can ruin you as much as make you. Stay away from Reggie or anybody else's clients. You broke the pact."

"I know."

"Don't forget again." And Rachael slammed down the phone.

---***---

Lamar was getting into his car at the diner. Rachael Short had pulled into the spot next to him and was just getting out.

"Good morning, Chief."

"How are you, Rachael?"

"I'm doing fine. Will I see you at the council meeting tomorrow night?"

"Of course. I'm always there to answer questions or to keep the peace."

"Any interesting things happening on the beach lately?"

"Oh, you know. The same things with the kids, but there have been some interesting developments with Marty McCabe's accident."

"What's that?"

"Well, I can't really talk about it. The Staties have taken another look at Marty's truck and took some things to the State Police lab for testing. I'll let you know when I hear back."

"I hope it's nothing that will embarrass poor old Marty."

"No. We wouldn't want to do that."

Chapter 24: Love the One You're With

Reggie met Sandra Fleming at a restaurant on Fenwick Island. They had made arrangements during the week after Reggie had called her. She didn't play hard to get and provided the time and place that they should meet. Reggie had driven south to Fenwick and Sandra had driven a few miles north from her place to the restaurant.

Reggie was downright giddy during the drive. He felt like a middle-schooler going to the seventh grade dance. It had been a while since he had dated anyone. He was always so busy. Now he had time but he was grossly out of practice. Sandra had certainly piqued his interest. She seemed realistic with no pretenses. It was refreshing. She also seemed interested and was very straightforward.

The hostess seated them at a table by a window overlooking the salt water inlet. They were toward the back of the restaurant and it was very quiet. Business was not brisk on a weeknight.

"I'm happy you called. I wasn't sure you would." She said reaching out for his hand across the table.

"After that parting gesture last Saturday, how could I not?" Reggie replied. He could still feel her lips on his...he was anxious that she might do that again.

Again, Sandra had not chosen a family restaurant but a quiet, fine dining establishment. The waiter with his white starched shirt, black bowtie, and black pants appeared. Greeting them warmly and offering the specials of the day.

"Let's order and talk some more. Do you mind if we get a bottle of white wine?"

"That sounds good. I was going to have seafood anyway."

Sandra ordered Dover sole and a bottle of Riesling. Reggie ordered the crab dish special. He wasn't particularly fond of crab but hey, Maryland was famous for them. The waiter brought the wine and poured some for them both to sample. They both nodded that it was good and the waiter filled their glasses, deposited the wine bottle in an ice bucket he had brought to the table, and disappeared.

And talk they did. They told each other about their lives and how they got to the place they were now filling in the blanks they had left from their previous evening together. The waiter delivered salad and then the main course. Dinner was wonderful and the conversation flowed easily and continuously between them. A few times during the meal, Sandra had reached for his hand across the table. Her touch lingered with a caressing motion that they both shared.

"I asked you last week if you believed in fate," Sandra asked.

"And I said I believed that things do just happen. We are where we are at a moment and that leads to what will happen. But we always have a choice to let it happen or pull back from it."

"Do you think something could happen with me and you?" Reggie asked. Sandra's leg and foot were now firmly entwined around Reggie's own and had been for a while.

"I'm here. You are here. And I definitely feel something happening." He left off the part that he would not pull back from it. Sandra's leg tightened around his own.

"So do I. Let's have dessert at my place."

Reggie quickly took care of the bill and followed Sandra to her condo building. He pulled into the parking garage behind her and took the spot next to her labeled "visitor" as she had told him. They both got out of their cars and as Reggie caught up to her, Sandra reached for his hand and they walked hand in hand to the elevator.

Once the elevator doors closed, she turned to him and took his other hand. She angled her face and looked into his eyes. Reggie may have been out of practice and maybe it had been a long time but he picked up on the queue and kissed her deeply. She leaned into him and returned the kiss, their lips gently moving in unison. It was all too brief as they parted as the elevator doors opened.

"Well, at least the "first kiss" nervousness is gone. Now, we can relax and look forward to more."

Reggie returned her smile, took her hand again, and walked with her to her condo located on the second floor and up a short flight of stairs behind the reception area. She said hello to the clerk on duty but did not linger. Reggie followed her up the stairs and they entered her unit.

"Come in...I'll get us some more wine. Did you like the Riesling?" she said turning to him.

"I liked it very much but there was something much sweeter that I liked more." Their hands were joined once more and the kiss was much longer and deeper this time. Sandra let go of Reggie's hands and wrapped her arms around him and softly caressed his neck.

Reggie was surely excited and breathing a bit hard. Sandra didn't seem to notice and was letting out soft noises as her own breathing quickened.

"It's been a while," she whispered as they broke the kiss but not the embrace.

"Me, too; but I don't think they have changed the rules."

"I don't think there are any more rules...at least not tonight," she said as she slipped off her sandals.

Sandra began to lead him toward the bedroom saying, "Do you want anything?"

"I do believe you know exactly what I want."

"Yes, I believe I do," she said as she unzipped her dress.

And they did have a very sweet "dessert" overlooking the Ocean City beach from her bedroom condo window where something most definitely did happen.

Chapter 25: The Ring of Fire

"I heard back from the Staties," the Chief said as they were seated in their usual morning booth at Stan & Ollie's.

"And what did they say," asked Reggie.

"Well, I gave them the bottle that you found and explained where you found it. They were not too happy that we hadn't put alcohol down as a contributing factor to the accident but they understood when I explained it to them. Seeing that the bottle broke in the course of the accident, they let it go. Then, they went through the car themselves, tearing it apart and taking what they wanted. I also told them about your observation about the speed."

"So, they are looking for other causes?" asked Joe.

"They took a bunch of stuff off of the truck with them back to the crime lab. The lab ran a bunch of tests and they did agree with you about the bottle breaking during the accident. They think Marty had it in his hand for some reason, but he obviously couldn't have been drinking it because it was still sealed."

"That eliminates alcohol as a contributing factor," said Joe.

"Did they find anything else?" asked Reggie.

"Yes, they did. They took the computer chip out of the car. I don't know how all this works but they said it had been replaced. They checked with the dealer and what was in the truck was not an approved part. They tested it somehow and said that if the cruise control was engaged, the accelerator would have gone to maximum and the brake pedal would no longer disengage the cruise control like it is supposed to. Essentially, the truck would have accelerated until the driver shut off the engine with the key."

They all sat and thought about that for a moment. Then Joe said, "So, if someone replaced the original computer chip with that one, they would create at least an unsafe situation, if not an unrecoverable and out of control vehicle."

"That's right Joe. That's what the Staties said. It was deliberately changed and nobody but Marty drove that truck. His wife had her own car. They think that once the truck left the road, Marty was so busy trying to control it, he never thought to shut off the engine."

"The person who replaced the chip killed Marty McCabe."

"...As if he had stabbed him in the heart."

---***---

"Girls, we've got a serious problem."

"How's that Rachael?" asked Kate.

"You all know we have the perfect situation here. The council votes on the Seaside Condo project tomorrow and the vote is all but a lock...right," Rachael addressing the group as she looked every one of the girls in the eye. No one else spoke. "But now we have a bit of a problem. The Chief told me that the State Police are looking at other causes for Marty McCabe's accident."

"What should that mean to us?" asked Candy.

"We weren't involved in that," said Sue.

"Well…we were trying to make sure we got approval on the Seaside project."

"Rachael, what do you mean we were trying to make sure?" asked Sue.

"We wanted the vote to go our way." Rachael was shrinking now. She did not sound as sure of herself as she usually did.

"What do you mean Rachael?" Candy asked sounding more confused.

Rachael had called this meeting to get the story straight, purposely leaving Jill McCabe out. She didn't want all that whining and crying to get in the way of containing the issue. They were in a spot and they had to act together to keep from losing control of the situation.

"She means, we kind of set Marty up," said Kate who was fidgeting and looking more nervous by the minute.

"Who's we? Who knew about this?" Candy again her voice getting louder.

"I didn't want to involve everybody so just Kate and I knew about it."

"Rachael, you and Kate have always been very close and we know you have been more than that, but what exactly have you done?" Candy had now reached a crescendo. Rachael knew she was going to lose it.

"We changed the computer chip in Marty's truck and made it go out of control," Kate blurted. "Rachael or I didn't do it, Alan did it for us," Kate completed the confession.

"You involved us in the murder of Marty, Jill's husband, just so we could get the vote on the Seaside Condo project," summarized Sue. She was now standing and pointing her finger at Rachael.

"Who has violated the code now?" asked Debbie looking directly at Rachael.

---***---

Lamar, Reggie, and Joe looked at each other. They were sitting in Joe's car with the listening device going on the dash. It was picking up the girls talking in Kate Leeman's house. Joe had left the microphone on the Leeman's window a couple of weeks before and never retrieved it. They had come from Stan & Ollie's, and parked down the street from the Leeman place when they saw all of the cars parked out front.

"Did I just hear what I thought I heard?"

"Yes, Reggie. That's a confession. The best evidence you can get."

"Is all that on tape?" asked the chief from the back seat.

"You bet," said Joe.

"Do you want to go in and arrest them now, Chief?"

"No. Let me get warrants to pick them up. Then I'll go to their homes individually. Maybe we'll get them to repeat this information. Then it will be admissible in court. I'm not sure what we have now is valid."

Chapter 26: Satisfaction

"Rachael, do you mind if we come in?"

Lamar, with two of his patrolmen, was standing on Rachael and Alan Short's porch. A State Police cruiser with two officers was parked by the curb. Rachael caught a glimpse of the Chief's backup and a look of concern, maybe more than concern, took hold of her.

"Of course, Lamar. What's this all about?" Rachael was making an effort to maintain her composure. Lamar and the two Bethany officers stepped inside leaving the door open.

"We have a warrant, but we don't want to make a scene," Chief Stanton said handing the document to Rachael. "Where is your husband...? Alan?" The Chief was looking into other rooms as they entered.

I'm right here Chief," Alan said as he came toward them from the kitchen.

"Why don't we all step into the sitting room," Rachael suggested.

Rachael took Alan's hand and led them all toward the sitting room. Chief Stanton took a chair, Alan and Rachael took the couch, and the two officers stood by the door.

"What's this all about," asked Alan. Looking perplexed on this face but the rest of his body showed the nervousness he was really feeling. Chief Stanton got up, walked over to the couch, and handed Alan the warrant. Alan reached for the document.

"That is a warrant for your arrest," announced the Chief pointing at the paper now in Alan's hands.

"Arrest! What the hell is this?" The Chief could now see as everyone else in the room, Alan's hands visibly shaking as he attempted to read the warrant.

"This will go easier if we all keep calm," the Chief said holding his hands out palms down.

"What is the charge?" it was Rachael asking in a shaky voice.

"Attempted murder and conspiracy for now," indicated the Chief sitting back in the chair.

"What have you got me into Rachael?" He looked directly at Rachael.

"Shut up Alan. Don't say anything."

"That could be good advice, Alan," said the Chief and he recited Miranda to both of them. "So you both understand?"

"Yes." said Rachael.

"I do understand, but Rachael you said..."

"Shut up Alan."

"No. I'm tired of listening to you. Look where it has landed me." Alan's voice was becoming louder as he spoke. "It was all your idea. I should never have listened to you; you and those bitches. I can't stand it anymore." And it didn't stop there. Rachael started wailing and the whole sorted tale came out of Alan.

Alan told of his wife's forcing him to contact a friend who was an electronics wizard for the chip to put in Marty McCabe's truck. That he had put it in days before but it only worked when the cruise control was engaged and they couldn't be certain when that would be or exactly what would happen. They only wanted to warn Marty and get him off the council.

Alan told of how Rachael and the rest of the Bethany Blues had set the whole thing up and they didn't care about Jill McCabe even if she happened to be in the truck when the chip was activated. He laid out the tactics the girls had used to get their way all stemming from that pact they made all those years ago. Rachael wailed, Alan talked, the names were revealed, and nothing was held back.

It was like Perry Mason had that pivotal witness on the stand and his detective Paul came in and whispered in his ear to give him the last piece of the puzzle to use in grilling the witness. And he took that bit and tricked the witness into telling all that they knew.

In the end, all of the Bethany Blues except for Jill McCabe, and Alan were taken into custody and were now guests of the county jail.

---***---

"Tell me. Tell me what happened," Lexie excitedly came to the table where Chief Stanton, Joe, and Reggie had just taken a seat.

"You should have seen it. It was glorious." The Chief recounted the whole tale of rounding up the Bethany Blues.

"What a scene. Was it the same at the other girls' homes?" asked Reggie.

"It was interesting, but not as fiery as at the Shorts," said the Chief.

"What happens now?"

"Their arraignment is set for Monday, but with what we have already there isn't much doubt as to their guilt. Some of the girls, I'm sure, will be material witnesses and turn state's evidence but Alan and Rachel will be headed for prison. Oh, and the council meeting set for tonight has been postponed."

"Sorry Reggie. It looks like you'll need a new real estate agent," said Joe.

"And have to start shopping all over again. Probably won't get in on the ground floor for the Seaside Condos either."

"I don't think anyone is ever moving into those," said Chief Stanton.

They finished their breakfast and had an extra cup of coffee. The Chief finally said he had to go to work and they walked out together. The Chief got into his car and Reggie and Joe walked to the band stand area and had a seat on one of the benches and stared at the dune in front of them.

"What are you going to do today," asked Joe.

"I think I'm going to get my book, sit in the lounge, and enjoy the ocean breezes."

"Is this seat taken...can we share your bench?" asked a pair of good looking brunettes.

Reggie and Joe looked at each other and started laughing.

"Sorry ladies. You can have the bench," Reggie said as they both got up. "Anyway, you can't see the ocean, and we have to go and take a nap."

About the Author

DJ Charpentier is a retired educator. Mr. Charpentier also served over twenty years in the Air National Guard. He has authored several long range plans for improving education, wrote for the base newspaper, and published squadron training plans. *As Luck Would Have It* was his first full length manuscript. *Bethany Blues* is his first work of fiction. Mr. Charpentier lives is Rhode Island and travels extensively with his wife in their motor home throughout the United States.

From the author:

I enjoy getting mail from readers and attempt to answer all Email. Please, do not send snail mail. With all the traveling we do, there is no way I can answer those promptly. If you do want an answer, please send Email to DPCharp@gmail.com; snail mail, no answer.

Writing is something I find extremely enjoyable and wish I had started writing fiction years ago. I enjoy reading because a well crafted story transports you to a place and immerses you in another world. Writing does the same except you can craft that world and manipulate the characters to fit what you wish to happen. It is a lot of work but the rewards outweigh the pain.

Many characters in this book, as do many of my song compositions, start out to be about a specific person; but surely do not end up that way. The characters in this book are pure fiction. If you think you are reading about yourself...look again...it's not you.

DJ Charpentier

Acknowledgement

I want to make mention of special thank you to my daughter Lori and my wife Pat. They have helped my effort to produce this book in several ways, some I may not fully understand or know. I do know that they both took the time to edit the content and make suggestions about this story. Thanks so much to both of you for having the patience to do that and to put up with me.

Made in the USA
Charleston, SC
13 June 2016

Made in the USA
Charleston, SC
13 June 2016